SMITTEN

WITH CROISSANTS

D1610569

A SWEET ROMANTIC COMEDY

SET IN FRANCE

ELLEN JACOBSON

Smitten with Croissants
Copyright © 2020 by Ellen Jacobson

Print ISBN: 978-1-951495-15-2
Digital ISBN: 978-1-951495-14-5
Large Print ISBN: 978-1-951495-16-9

Editor: By the Book Editing
Cover Design: Melody Jeffries Design

First Printing: February 2021

Published by: Ellen Jacobson
www.ellenjacobsonauthor.com

For those of you out there who adore reading geeky love stories while devouring so many buttery, flaky croissants that you end up with a tummy ache but you don't care because they're so darn delicious.

CONTENTS

CHAPTER 1
SMOOCHY FACE

"For crying out loud, this is a buffet line, not some nightclub," I mutter under my breath. "Go play smoochy face someplace else."

My friend, Isabelle, glances at me. "Smoochy face? What are you talking about, Mia?"

I point at a young couple engaged in a full-on make-out session and pull a face. "No one wants to see that while they're waiting to eat. Why did they even bother coming on a cruise if all they're going to do is grope each other? They should have stayed home. Or, at the very least, inside their cabin."

Isabelle laughs. "You really aren't a fan of public displays of affection, are you?"

"That's not true," I protest.

She arches an eyebrow. "Hmm . . . I seem to remember the time your boyfriend tried to hold your hand in public. You almost decapitated him with that sword of yours."

"First of all, he wasn't my boyfriend. I only went on a few dates with him. A few too many, I might add." I put my hands on my hips. "Second, it's a *lightsaber*, not a sword. And third, his hand was all gross and sweaty."

"Gross and sweaty, huh? So that's why you stabbed him?"

"I did not stab him . . . At least not on purpose. Listen, all I did was try to pull my hand away. But then I lost my balance and tripped, and that's when my lightsaber accidentally smacked into his neck."

"Good thing it's made of plastic, otherwise you could have done some serious damage to his carotid artery."

"I guess." I purse my lips. "Unfortunately, I can't afford one of those custom-made steel lightsabers with a titanium handle."

Isabelle rolls her eyes. "Did you ever think that perhaps you're a tad bit over obsessed with *Star Wars*?"

I ignore her jibe, instead nodding toward the couple holding up the line. "Geez, look at where his hands are now. If he moves them any more, we're going to find out what color her underwear is any second now."

"Hmm, you might be right. Her skirt is pretty short. Doesn't really fit the 1950s theme for tonight's dinner. Miniskirts weren't a thing until the sixties." Isabelle toys with her pearl necklace. "But I guess it's pretty hard to pack for all the themed events they have planned for the cruise."

"Well, if I managed it, anyone can."

Isabelle snorts. "That's true. You are one of the most disorganized people I've ever met."

"I'm not disorganized. I'm creative. Completely different." I shake my head as the couple continues to hold up the line. Standing on my tiptoes, I wave my hands over my head at them. "Hey, knock it off or get a room. Some of us want to eat tonight."

Isabelle grabs my arm and pulls me back. "Shush. They'll hear you."

"That's the point."

"The line's moving now. You can cool your jets."

"My jets are just fine, thank you very much."

Isabelle scoffs, then turns and smiles at the girl in line behind us. It's one of those smiles that says, "Please ignore my friend. She's constantly embarrassing me."

The girl smiles back. I'm pretty sure her smile means, "Your friend is totally right about that couple. I admire her for saying out loud what the rest of us were thinking." At least, I'd like to think that's what it means. Who knows, maybe she was just smiling about the fact that they're serving two kinds of coleslaw tonight. People can get excited about that kind of thing.

"Looks like we shop at the same place," Isabelle says to the girl.

It's true. She's dressed similarly to us with a full skirt, gloves, and pearls. As I admire her auburn curls, which are tucked underneath a broad-brimmed hat, I toy with a strand of my long blonde hair, trying to decide if I would look good as a redhead.

After we introduce ourselves—the other girl's name is Ginny—I turn my attention back to the line in front of me. It still hasn't moved an inch while the lovebirds continue to express their desire for each other for all the world to see.

Oh, by the way, Miss Lovebird's underwear is pink. Way more information than you or the rest of us waiting in line probably want to know.

"Excuse me." An older woman standing behind the couple taps the man on his shoulder.

They pull back from each other, just now seeming to notice where they are— on the lido deck of a cruise ship making a transatlantic crossing from Miami to Europe.

"You must be newlyweds," the woman says to them. "I remember when my Ernie and I got married forty years ago. We couldn't keep our hands off each other either."

After some inane chitchat between the three of them about flower girls and ring bearers, the line finally moves forward.

I grab a plate, but as I turn to pass it to Isabelle, it slips out of my hands and crashes on the floor, shattering into pieces.

A waiter rushes over. As he bends down to clean up the mess, the collar of his white shirt pulls back, and I can see something that looks like a tattoo at the base of his neck. I lean forward to get a closer look, when he suddenly shifts position, bumping his head against my arm.

I startle as I realize that my fingers are lightly brushing his hair. His impossibly soft, sandy-brown hair. The dude has some great conditioning products going on.

He stands and I quickly take a step backward, putting my hands behind my back.

"Sorry about the plate."

"*Ne soyez pas désolée,*" he says, his hazel eyes twinkling. "*Je voulais vous rencontrer depuis que vous êtes montée à bord du navire.*"

My jaw drops as I watch him walk

away. I know that my French is rusty, but did he just say that he had been looking for an excuse to meet me since I boarded the ship? And did he wink at me?

"You're kind of a klutz today," Isabelle jokes, snapping me back to reality. "First you spilled perfume in our cabin and now this."

"It's these stupid gloves. They're slippery," I say as I yank them off. "How did anyone manage to get anything done back in the fifties wearing these things?"

"They probably are a safety hazard." Ginny pulls her gloves off as well then looks at them. "Now what do I do with them? I don't have any pockets, and I didn't bring a purse."

I grin and stick my gloves down the front of my sweater. "That's what bras are for," I say. "They're great for holding your phone and money, along with gloves when you don't have any other way to carry them."

Ginny grins back and stuffs her gloves down her sweater. Isabelle frowns. I wonder if she's going to join in—drawing attention to herself is something she generally avoids. But after a moment, she joins the bra-stuffing brigade.

The three of us giggle about our lopsided cleavage as we pile hamburgers, hot dogs, corn on the cob, two kinds of coleslaw, and deviled eggs on our plates.

"Are you traveling on your own?" Isabelle asks Ginny.

"I am," she says.

"Come sit with us," Isabelle says.

"Oh, yes, join us," I say. "But only on one condition. No talking about guys."

"Mia just had a bad break-up," Isabella says.

"Bad?" I scowl. "Bad is what you say when you're describing the taste of beetroots. My mother would wash my mouth out with soap if I use a word that really describes what happened, so I won't. You'll just have to trust me, it was a lot worse than eating beetroots."

Ginny sets her plate down. "You won't get any argument from me. The last thing I want to talk about is guys. Besides, I hate beetroots too."

"Cool. Let's talk about why these petticoats itch so much instead. What I wouldn't give for a pair of yoga pants right now."

"Me too. I could live in my yoga pants twenty-four seven," Isabelle says. "But despite the gloves and the petticoats, you have to admit traveling to Europe on a cruise ship is heavenly. It sure beats flying."

I shudder. "I hate flying."

"That makes two of us," Ginny says.

"Make that three," Isabelle adds. "I couldn't believe my luck when I won two free tickets on this cruise ship. Mia and I were just about to book flights to Europe when it happened."

"It sure beats flying," I say. "But I would have sucked it up and gotten on a plane if I had to. Nothing is going to get in the way of what I want to achieve."

"What do you want to achieve?" Ginny asks before taking a sip of her milkshake.

"World domination," I say. "Isn't that every girl's dream?"

* * *

"World domination?" Ginny chuckles. "I'm not sure I could handle managing an entire planet. I'd be happy just knowing what I want to do with my life."

"Really? I've known what I want to do with my life since I was a little girl," I say.

"Mia is very goal oriented," Isabelle says.

"I used to be goal oriented too," Ginny

says. "But then my world got turned upside down by a jerk. Now, I'm rethinking everything."

I lean forward. "Same. Except the rethinking part. I still know what I want to do, but after a guy screwed up my life, it kind of threw a monkey in the wrench."

"That doesn't make sense," Isabelle says. "How can you throw a monkey in the wrench? Why would you throw a monkey in the first place?"

"It's an expression," I say. "You know, from the movie *Die Hard*. Don't you remember the scene where Bruce Willis' character said, 'Just a fly in the ointment, a monkey in the wrench, a pain in the—"

Isabelle holds up her hand. "Please, no more Bruce Willis quotes." She turns to Ginny. "She's obsessed with Bruce Willis. It's almost as bad as her obsession with *Star Wars*."

"Am not," I say.

"Are too," Isabelle retorts.

Fortunately, Ginny intervenes and changes the subject, telling us that the original expression, "throw a monkey wrench in the works," dates back to the early 1900s when people threw tools inside industrial machinery as an act of sabotage.

During dinner, she shares other historical trivia, including the fact that ancient Romans used to eat while reclining on couches. Totally my kind of people. It's good to know that there's a historical precedent for all the times I lie on my sofa in my yoga pants while eating pizza.

After we polish off our hamburgers and hot dogs, I bring back dessert for everyone at the table.

"We can eat this without feeling guilty," I say, setting the tray down. "Angel food cake isn't made with butter or oil."

Isabelle shakes her head. "How many

calories does that have?"

"Does what have?" I ask.

"That shake, silly."

I wave my hand hypnotically in front of Isabelle's face. "This isn't the shake you're looking for."

She snorts. "Your Jedi mind tricks aren't going to work on me. Or on your hips. That shake is real, sweetie."

I roll my eyes while Isabelle tells Ginny about how she convinced me to leave my lightsaber at home. Little does she know that I packed a Princess Leia costume. I'm positive it will come in handy at some point.

When Ginny says that she doesn't really like *Star Wars* movies, I gasp.

"I'm more into documentaries," she says. "You know, stuff that's real."

I gulp down the rest of my milkshake, astonished that anyone would think that the Force isn't real.

"Is anyone sitting here, girls?"

I look up and see the older woman

who intervened and got the annoying couple to stop playing smoochy face at the buffet long enough for the rest of us to get our dinner.

"It's free," Ginny says. "Please have a seat, ma'am."

"We'll have none of that 'ma'am' nonsense," she says, wagging a finger. "That makes me feel positively ancient. The name's Celeste."

After we introduce ourselves, I get teary-eyed as Celeste toys with her wedding ring and tells us about her late husband, Ernie. Marriage suits some people. Not me, though. Not gonna happen. Not ever. Never ever . . . again.

Yeah, that's right. I was married once. And trust me, once is enough.

I surreptitiously wipe my eyes, then change the subject, asking Celeste if she travels a lot.

"Oh, yes," she says. "This is day four hundred and ninety-eight of my world travels. Or is that four hundred and ninety-nine days?" She shakes her head, trying to do the math involved with changing time zones. "Anyway, I'm headed to Greece next. What about you girls? Where are you going?"

Ginny tells us that she's disembarking in Rome, then taking a train to Ravenna.

"We're getting off in Rome too," Isabelle says. "After that, it's all up in the air. The only thing I know is that I have to be in Cologne by the beginning of July. I've got a job working on one of those German river cruise boats lined up."

Celeste nods, then looks at me.

"I'm going to head to Paris and get a job at an art gallery," I say with more confidence than I feel.

"Mia is a really talented artist," Isabelle says.

"Oh, I'd love to see your paintings," Celeste says. "What do you work in? Oils? Acrylics? Watercolors?"

"Ink," I say.

"That sounds fascinating. I have a friend who does these wonderful pen and ink drawings of her cats. What kind of paper do you use?"

"Uh, the kind made of human cells."

Celeste looks alarmed. "Human cells?"

"She's a tattoo artist," Isabelle explains. "Emphasis on artist. She does replicas of the great masters' work. You should see the tattoo she recently did of one of Van Gogh's sunflower paintings on this guy's back."

"It would have worked better if he hadn't kept squirming. One of the sunflowers turned out looking more like a turnip."

When Ginny asks me about my own tattoos, I laugh. "Me? Are you kidding? I would never get a tattoo. I'm scared of needles."

"Ah, aichmophobia," she says. "That's more common than you'd think."

I furrow my brow. "Ach-a-what?"

An older gentleman interrupts before Ginny can explain. He asks if any of us would care to dance, but it's obvious he only has eyes for Celeste. As he escorts her to the dance floor, she says over her shoulder, "Don't go anywhere. After this dance, I want to talk with Mia about getting a tattoo."

"What kind of tattoo do you think she wants?" Ginny asks.

"Maybe something that reminds her of her husband," Isabelle says.

I watch as Celeste's dance partner twirls her around. "I'm not so sure about that. He's been gone for over a year. Maybe it's time for her to move on."

Isabelle looks at me thoughtfully. "Maybe it's time for you to move on too."

* * *

After dinner, Isabelle and Ginny went to watch a Broadway revue. I begged off.

I'd rather get a tattoo then listen to chirpy performers sing show tunes.

Instead, I go out on deck and lean over the railing, looking at the moonlight reflecting on the water. How in the world am I going to find a job at an art gallery in Paris? The French have a reputation for being aloof, especially in the art world. It's doubtful they're going to welcome an American girl like me into their fold.

I run my fingers through my hair and admonish myself. "Stop with the negative thoughts, Mia. Just because your family doesn't believe in you, doesn't mean you won't succeed."

When I announced my plans to my parents, they'd scoffed. They couldn't understand why anyone would want to leave the small town that I had grown up in, let alone go abroad.

"They eat snails in France," my mother said, wrinkling her nose.

"You mean *escargot*?" I asked.

"Es … es ..." My father scowled as he struggled with the pronunciation. "Why can't they just say snails like normal people? Why can't they eat normal food like pot roast?"

"*Escargot* is French for snails," I explained. "They're served in garlic butter. You like garlic bread, Dad. Maybe you'd like *escargot* too."

He folded his arms across his chest. "Only an idiot would eat a common garden pest, garlic butter or no garlic butter. I bet they serve those es... es … snails at that fancy country club where you used to be a waitress. It's exactly the type of thing rich people would pay top dollar for."

"Well, then I must be an idiot because I plan on ordering a big plate of them when I get to Paris." While I sounded defiant when I uttered this, inwardly I was shuddering. The thought of eating snails makes me queasy, but there was no way I was going to let my parents know that.

The sound of high heels clicking on the deck interrupts my thoughts. "There you are," Celeste says as she walks toward me. "I've been looking for you everywhere."

I cock my head to one side. "What's up?"

"Let's talk tattoos," she says. "It's on my bucket list, but I can't decide what to get, let alone where to get it. At my age, I have my fair share of wrinkles. Can you tattoo over wrinkles? What about saggy skin? Am I too old to get a tat? That's what you say, right? Tats?"

"You're never to old to get a tat," I say with a smile. "Did you know that Judi Dench got her first one at eighty-one? And you're way younger than she is."

"Ooh . . . I love Judi Dench." Celeste squeezes my arm. "You've convinced me. Let's do it."

"What? Here on the cruise ship?"

"Sure, why not?"

"Uh . . . well . . . you probably need some sort of special license."

"If the captain can marry people at sea, I'm sure a little old tattoo wouldn't be a problem. Come on, we can get set up back in my suite."

I grin at her enthusiasm. "Unfortunately, I didn't bring my equipment with me. You need a special machine and needles, not to mention ink. Besides, you should really think about it carefully before you go ahead. It's not something you can undo easily."

"Nope, my mind is made up. When I know what I want, I go for it. Just like I did with my Ernie when I first laid eyes on him." Celeste rests her hands on the railing, closes her eyes, and breathes in the sea air deeply. "I wish he could be here now. He would have loved to go on a cruise."

"Why didn't you ever take one with him?"

"Well, when we first got married, we

were completely broke. Besides, cruises weren't really a thing back then like they are now. Later, when we had more money, we didn't have the time. Or rather, we didn't make the time. That's what's nice about seeing you young people having adventures now before you get married and settle down."

I chew my lip. "It almost didn't work out that way for me."

Celeste turns her head and looks at me. "What do you mean?"

"When I was twenty, I almost settled down. Thankfully, it didn't work out."

"You were engaged?"

"More than engaged. I was married."

"Really? For how long?"

"Less than twenty-four hours."

She raises her eyebrows. "That's a short marriage. What happened?"

"His parents happened," I say bitterly. "They were dead set against me from day one. I wasn't good enough for their precious boy."

"But they must have come around in the end. The two of you got married."

"No, they completely freaked out when he told them that he wanted to propose to me, so we ended up eloping. When they found out what we had done, they hit the roof. They threatened to disown him."

"Were they serious?" Celeste asks. "I can't imagine any parents wanting to cut off contact with their child."

"They had threatened to disown him before, when we were dating, but we never thought they would go through with it . . ." My voice cracks as I recall the phone conversation with them. Then I straighten my shoulders and continue. "The family lawyer tracked us down hours after our wedding ceremony and insisted on a private conversation with my husband. After about an hour, the lawyer handed me a letter."

"The lawyer? What happened to your husband?"

"He left." I snap my fingers. "One minute we were happy newlyweds, looking forward to our honeymoon. The next minute, he had vanished, and I was all alone."

"What did the letter say?"

"A whole bunch of legal mumbo-jumbo which boiled down to one thing—my marriage was over. My husband chose his family fortune over me."

"Oh, sweetie, you poor thing." Celeste squeezes my hand. "I can't imagine why anyone would choose money over you. Why wouldn't his parents have approved of you? It makes no sense."

I take a deep breath. "Oh, it's the usual story—a girl from the wrong side of the tracks. They assumed I was a gold digger, just out for their son's money. What they didn't realize was that I was marrying him *despite* his money, and his parents, and all of their country club connections."

"It sounds like you're better off without

him and his family. Money isn't everything." Celeste gets a faraway look in her eyes. "There was a guy who was sweet on me once. He was loaded, but I never could have been with him."

"Because he was rich?"

She laughs. "No, I didn't mind the money. It was *how* he made his money. Not exactly on the up-and-up, if you know what I mean. But it all worked out in the end. I met my Ernie a few years later, and he turned out to be the love of my life. He was the guy I was meant to be with all along. You'll see. The same thing will happen to you. You'll meet a good man who will stand up for you against anything, and anyone."

I shake my head firmly. "I don't ever plan on falling in love again, let alone getting married. Once was enough."

"Was your marriage annulled? If so, it's like you get a do-over."

"Just because you get an annulment doesn't mean it didn't happen." I clench my fists. "What kind of stupid rule is that, anyway? If you're going to put on a white dress and have a minister marry you, you're married. Even if it only lasts for less than twenty-four hours. If I ever get a tattoo, it would say..." My voice trails off as I feel my nails digging into the palms of my hands.

"Say what?" Celeste asks.

"Never mind," I say, slowly unclenching my fists. "It's not like I'm going to get a tattoo, anyway. They're too permanent."

Celeste furrows her brow. "That's odd, considering you're a tattoo artist."

I grin. "That's me . . . odd. Anyway, let's talk about your tattoo. There are all different kinds of styles to choose from. I can show you some pictures."

She nods. "That sounds like a good idea. I know that I want it to say 'floss' but I'm not sure what style to do it in."

"Floss? That's cute. Is it a nickname? What Ernie called you?"

Celeste looks at me blankly. "Nickname? No, 'floss' as in 'floss your teeth.' I figure it would be a good reminder."

"You want to tattoo a reminder about...dental hygiene on your body?" I stammer. "Wouldn't it be easier to tape a note on the mirror?"

"No, don't be silly. I'd never notice that. But something tattooed, well, I'd see that every day when I get out of the shower."

"You sure you don't want something like a flower or a rose, maybe? Or a cat? Cats are really popular."

"No, dear. I'm going to go with 'floss.' It's far more practical than a tattoo of a cat."

I rub my temples. This is possibly the strangest tattoo that I've ever heard, and I've heard some real doozies. "Did you have any other ideas?"

"Well, sometimes I forget to take my blood pressure pills and there's the issue with my dishwasher—"

Before she can tell me what kind of dishwasher-related tattoo she's considering, we're interrupted by a commotion on the deck below us. I lean over the railing and see a woman jabbing her finger at a waiter while complaining at the top of her lungs about the fact that her strawberry daiquiri tastes like . . . wait for it . . . strawberries.

I've dealt with her type before when I was a waitress at the country club. I'm impressed with how the waiter is managing to keep his cool. If this happened to me, I would have told the obnoxious lady exactly where to go. The kind of place that's hot all year round, if you get my drift. Keeping my mouth shut was never my strong suit. Probably explains why my waitressing gig only lasted three days. Longer than my marriage, so there is that.

The woman shoves the glass into the

waiter's hands, sloshing its contents everywhere. As she storms off, I call out, "Hey, aren't you going to clean that up, lady?"

I gasp as the waiter looks up. It's the same guy from earlier in the evening. The one with the sandy-brown hair that's softer than kitten fur. I feel my face grow warm as he locks his hazel eyes with mine.

"Who's that?" Celeste whispers. "He's cute."

"I have no idea," I say softly.

"I think you better find out," she says. "Because I'm pretty sure he just winked at you."

CHAPTER 2
SWEATY HANDS AND RUTABAGAS

A few days later, I'm lounging in a deck chair, a stack of glossy magazines and an iced tea on the table next to me. We're about a third of the way through our transatlantic crossing, and I'm already bored out of my mind. Not being able to see anything on the horizon other than endless water isn't helping my mood either. I almost wish I had flown instead . . . almost.

"I'm fed up with magazines trying to

tell me what to do and what I should look like," I mutter, flipping through an article dedicated to the latest weight loss fads. "Rutamentals? A diet based on rutabagas, guaranteed to help you lose those unwanted pounds? That sounds disgusting. I'm happy with my curves, thank you very much."

After flinging that magazine on the deck, I pick up another one and thumb through it. "Five steps to getting a boyfriend...ridiculous. How about five steps to making sure you *don't* get a boyfriend? That would be more far more useful."

I take a sip of my tea while I ponder what my anti-boyfriend steps would be. "Let's see, first, you have to avoid eye contact at all costs. Guys have been known to hypnotize you with their eyes. It's like a superpower. Whether they're baby blues, or deep, dark eyes framed with long eyelashes, or a pair of hazel eyes which are mischievously winking at you—"

I pause as a woman walking past looks sharply at me. Oops. I guess I've been talking out loud to myself. I do that sometimes. Sure, it might be a little weird, but I don't care what anyone thinks of me, least of all some snobby lady whose first word as a child was probably "tsk-tsk."

After a few moments, I realize that I'm not talking out loud anymore. Instead, all I'm doing is thinking about hazel eyes. Hazel eyes with a twinkle in them. Or, to be more specific, a cute French waiter with broad shoulders, hair you want to run your fingers through, and mesmerizing hazel eyes that just happen to be winking at me.

I mentally shake myself. Why in the world am I thinking about *him?* I haven't even seen the guy since the first night of the cruise. I don't even know his name. I don't want to know his name. I don't want to know anything about him.

This brings me to step number two—when you find yourself thinking about a guy, distract yourself with . . . well, with anything. I tend to think about the state of my cuticles.

After deciding I should apply some cuticle remover later, I grab the health and fitness magazine back off the deck and try to engross myself in diet recipes. Who knew you could puree cooked rutabaga and tofu, put it in the freezer for a few hours, and then pass it off as ice cream to unsuspecting dinner guests?

I glance up and see Isabelle effortlessly jogging toward me like a gazelle, her long ponytail swinging back and forth. She's smiling blissfully—the endorphins from her runner's high have clearly kicked in. Ginny is trailing behind her, shuffling from side to side like a duck waddling toward a pond. She's grimacing while she gasps for breath. Definitely no endorphins happening there.

Isabelle gives me a quick wave as she passes. Ginny tries to do likewise, but as she reaches her arm out, her hand gets caught in a life ring mounted on the railing. While trying to extract it, she trips over the stack of magazines on the deck, flies into me, and knocks me to the ground.

"Permettez-moi, mademoiselle."

I look up and see Mr. Hazel Eyes holding out his hand to help me up.

I'm torn. What if his hands are sweaty and gross? How disappointing would that be? Cute guys shouldn't have gross, sweaty hands—although in my experience they usually do. I'm confident that statistics will back me up on this. But, on the other hand, what if his hands are pleasantly dry? Don't I owe it to science to find out if he's a statistical anomaly?

"Mademoiselle?"

Science wins. I place my hand in his

and gasp. Not only are they dry, they're emitting some sort of weird energy particles that are causing my entire body to tingle from the tips of my fingers —which he's lightly caressing—down to the soles of my feet. The whole tingling thing is another one of those superpowers that the opposite sex use on us to make us swoon.

As he helps me to my feet, I wonder what these energy particles are. Could this be related to the legendary Force from *Star Wars*?

I quickly pull my hand away, avert my eyes, and try to distract myself by thinking about rutabaga and tofu ice cream.

The waiter furrows his brow. "*Vous allez bien*?"

"I'm fine, thanks," I say.

"I am very glad to hear that," he responds in perfect English, spoken with a swoon-worthy British accent. He scoops up the magazines strewn across the deck. As he hands the stack to me, he points at the headline promising five easy steps to get a man in your life. "Is this how you got your boyfriend?"

"Me? Boyfriend?" I stammer, clutching the magazines against my chest. "What boyfriend?"

His only response is a lazy grin.

"I don't have a boyfriend."

He nods slowly. "Hmm . . . no boyfriend. Interesting."

I scowl. This topic of conversation is *far* from interesting. Time to set Mr. Hazel Eyes straight. I shuffle through the magazines, find the article I'm looking for, then thrust it at him. "This is why I bought this—because of this photo shoot."

He cocks his head to one side. "Wedding dresses? That *is* interesting."

I feel my face grow warm. "No, it's not about the dresses. It's about the tattoos. See how each of the brides has a tattoo? They were done by Dominic de

Santis. He's the go-to guy when celebrities are looking to get some ink. He's an incredible artist."

"I'd love to get something like that one day." He points at a close-up picture of one of the brides' hands.

I quirk an eyebrow and say with a slight smirk, "A bouquet or a diamond solitaire engagement ring?"

"No, the tribal tattoo on her wrist. But, I'm afraid my employer wouldn't approve."

"But you already have a tattoo?"

He frowns. "How do you know that?"

"Um . . . I saw it the other night when you were cleaning up the plate I dropped."

He rubs his hand on the back of his neck, worry creasing his brow. "I didn't think anyone could see it."

"I don't think anyone can normally," I say. "It was the way you were positioned underneath me. Your shirt was pulled back and I could see some black ink."

I feel flustered as I remember that tantalizing bit of ink. What does the rest of his tattoo look like? How far down his back does it go? What does his back look like?

I mentally shake myself and continue, "Most people wouldn't have noticed. If they did, they probably thought it was dirt. Not that anyone would think you have dirt on your neck. I mean, that would be strange. Why would you have dirt on your neck? No, I'm sure no one could see it. The only reason I noticed was because—"

Someone clears their throat, interrupting my train of thought, which is probably a good thing because I was starting to babble.

"Uh, excuse me. I could use a little help down here."

I glance down and see Ginny lying on the deck, her hand pressed against her ankle.

"Oh, my gosh. I'm so sorry," I quickly say as I bend down next to her. "Are you okay?"

"I think I twisted my ankle."

"I'll summon the doctor," Mr. Hazel Eyes says in a smooth, professional tone.

"No, that's not necessary," Ginny says firmly. "Just help me up. I'm sure I'll be fine."

After the two of us assist her to her feet, and she reassures us that she's fine, the waiter—whose name I still don't know—excuses himself to take a drink order from a nearby couple.

Ginny nearly collapses as she tries to put her weight on her ankle.

"Maybe we should see that doctor," I say.

"I think you're right," Ginny says. "Where did your friend go?"

"My friend?" I say. "He's not my friend. He's just a . . . a . . . um . . . waiter."

Ginny smiles. "Okay, maybe he's not

your friend. But he's definitely not *just* a waiter. Unless, waiters usually wink at you like that."

* * *

Ginny slings her arm around my shoulders, and I help her hobble to the doctor's office. Actually, I'm not sure that I'm any help given how much shorter I am than her. Because Ginny has to lean down at an awkward angle for me to support her, I worry that the two of us are going to topple over again and land on the floor.

Fortunately, we reach the elevator without an incident and the doors glide open as soon as I press the button. Unfortunately, Mr. and Mrs. Smoochy Face are inside the elevator car, locked in a tight embrace while they make gooey eyes at each other, and completely blocking our way.

I clear my throat to get their attention,

but they're oblivious.

"Excuse me," Ginny says.

There's no response to her polite request.

"Hey, we're trying to get on," I say more forcefully.

Still no response.

As the elevator doors start to close, I hurl my stack of magazines in their direction. That finally gets their attention. They shuffle over a few steps, still glued together, and Ginny and I manage to squeeze in behind them.

"Give us some sugar, my little petunia," the guy says, leaning down to kiss his bride.

"Petunia?" She giggles. At least I think it's a giggle. The sound reminds me of my childhood pet guinea pig when he was demanding a carrot.

"You don't like petunia?" He pulls her closer to him. "Okay, how about my little mother of dragons?"

She giggles again as he nuzzles her

neck.

I groan. They've completely ruined *Game of Thrones* for me. How can I ever watch that again without thinking of squeaky guinea pigs engaging in way too much PDA?

"My little banana muffin?" he suggests, turning his body so that we have a close-up view of their lips locking. "My little baby cake?"

I gag while saying a prayer to the elevator gods. *Please, please don't let the elevator break down.* Someone is going to get hurt if I'm stuck in here with these two.

Finally, we reach our floor and the doors open.

After I help Ginny out, I turn to them. "If you want my opinion, I think you should go with 'my little guinea pig.'"

"Oh, that's cute," the girl squeaks.

As the doors shut behind us, I look at Ginny. "Some people just don't seem to get sarcasm."

She looks at me quizzically.

"I'll explain later," I say. "First, let's get you to the clinic."

While we wait for the doctor, Ginny chews on her lip as she scrolls through old texts from her ex-boyfriend.

"Why do you keep torturing yourself?" I ask. "You need to forget about him."

"Easier said than done." She shoves her phone back into the pocket of her sweatshirt. "It seems like everywhere I look there are reminders of him. My mom thinks I should start dating again. Casual dates with nice guys to help take my mind off what happened."

"Hmm . . . I'm not sure that works. My friends are constantly trying to set me up, but I feel like I'm wasting my time. All guys are the same—focused on money."

"How so?"

"They're either rich already—you know, stuck-up country club types—or they're obsessed with climbing the career ladder so that they can buy a big house and expensive car. They can't understand how I can be happy working at a tattoo parlor and why I'd rather talk about art than designer purses. Even worse, most of them have sweaty hands."

"Sounds like you're not dating the right kind of guys. Maybe you should go for something different. Someone who doesn't have a corporate job. What about that waiter you were flirting with earlier?"

I raise my eyebrows. "Flirting? Me? No way. Never."

Ginny rubs her ankle and smiles. "Uh-huh."

"I'm serious. I'm not one of those girls who bats her eyelashes, makes gooey eyes at a guy, or, worse yet, giggles when he calls her a silly pet name."

The nurse interrupts us. "The doctor is ready for you now."

"You sure about those gooey eyes?"

Ginny says over her shoulder as she limps into the doctor's office. "I saw how you were looking at that waiter—positively gooey."

"Was not," I mutter at her retreating back.

* * *

While I wait for Ginny, I pass the time reading magazines. They're full of ridiculous articles—like how to sculpt your glutes while mopping the floor, melting down crayons to make the ultimate hostess gifts, and decorating your hamster's cage for Halloween. It's a relief when Ginny finally appears in the reception area, leaning on a cane.

I jump up to help her. "What did the doctor say?"

"He thinks I just twisted it. Should be okay in a day or two with some rest. I need to ice it to bring down the swelling."

"Let's get you back to your cabin."

As we walk toward the elevators, Isabelle rushes up to us.

"Are you okay, Ginny? I had no idea you were hurt until Pierre told me."

"Who's Pierre?" I ask.

"You know Pierre." Isabelle turns and points at a guy standing at the end of the hallway.

"Hey, it's the winking waiter," Ginny says under her breath, giving me a sideways glance.

Pierre gives Isabelle a small wave. She motions him toward us. "Don't be shy. Come join us."

Ginny grins. "Shy? He's not shy. At least not with Mia."

"Shush," I say, giving her a nudge.

As Pierre approaches us, he smiles at me, his eyes twinkling. Worried that this twinkle might turn into a wink, I avert my eyes and carefully study the carpeted floor. It's not helpful. The plaid pattern is made up of slate blue, dark green, and deep brown colors—the exact hues in Pierre's hazel eyes. Why couldn't the cruise line have picked something in pinks and purples instead?

"How is your ankle, *mademoiselle*?" I hear Pierre asking Ginny.

"It's okay. Mia's helping me back to my cabin so that I can elevate my leg."

I look up sharply. Why did she have to tell him my name?

"May I be of any assistance?" he offers.

Ginny gives me a mischievous glance, then says brightly, "Maybe you can walk with us and make sure we get there okay?"

"I think we can find our way back by ourselves," I say. "It's not like we need help pushing elevator buttons."

"Oh, I'm an excellent button pusher," Pierre says. "I would be happy to escort you ladies."

"Great," Ginny says.

She and Isabelle take the lead, with

Pierre and I trailing behind. When we reach the elevator bank, I bite back a smile as Pierre dramatically presses the button.

"How do you girls know each other?" he asks while we wait for the elevator car.

"Mia and I have been friends forever," Isabelle says. "We met at the—"

I hold up my hand and give her a warning look. "I'm sure he doesn't want *all* the details."

"I can't believe you're still embarrassed about what happened," she says to me. Before I can protest, she continues. "Anyway, never mind how we met. The important thing is that she saved me from making a fool out of myself. She's always been there for me. I couldn't ask for a better friend."

My first instinct is to roll my eyes at Isabelle's sappiness. But when she puts her arm around my shoulders and gives me a sideways hug, I get misty-eyed.

Thankfully, the elevator arrives, and everyone is distracted while I dab my eyes.

"It's pretty full," Isabelle says. "Should we wait for the next one?"

Ginny shakes her head. "Nah. We'll take this one. Pierre and Mia can grab the next one."

"Good idea," Isabelle chimes in.

For someone with a twisted ankle, Ginny seems pretty spry as she hops into the elevator car before I can. She and Isabelle give us a cheeky wave as the doors close, pleased with their scheme to stick me with Pierre.

I scowl at them, then study the carpet again. For some unknown reason, the stupid hazel-colored plaid reminds me of what Pierre said to me on the first night of the cruise. Studiously avoiding eye contact with him, I casually ask, "That night at the buffet, what did you mean when you said you had been looking for an excuse to meet me? At least that's what I think you said. My French is pretty rusty."

"No, you got it right. That's what I said."

"Uh, okay, but what did you mean by it?"

"Oh, it was your *Star Wars* backpack. I wanted to know where you got it."

I give Pierre a sideways glance. "You're a *Star Wars* fan?"

"Guilty."

I look back down at the carpet, feeling oddly conflicted. On one hand, I'm glad the only reason he wanted to meet me was to geek out about *Star Wars*. But, on the other hand, I'm kind of disappointed that it was my backpack he was interested in . . . not me.

After a few moments, Pierre suggests that we take the stairs. "The elevators are busy this time of day."

I shrug. "I can find my own way. You probably need to go do waiter stuff."

"It's no problem. I'm off duty." He cups

my elbow with his hand and guides me toward the stairwell. "Besides, it's a good chance for me to get you alone."

My stomach flutters. "Alone?"

"Uh-huh. Isabelle told me that you're a tattoo artist. I want to get your opinion on a tattoo I'm thinking of getting."

When I realize that it's my professional opinion he wants, the stomach-fluttering stops. "The tribal one from the magazine? I thought you couldn't have one on your wrist?"

He holds the door to the stairwell open for me. "No, this would be on my back. Easier to hide."

As I walk down the stairs, I say over my shoulder, "I guess you can't take your shirt off then if you want to keep it a secret."

He doesn't respond until we reach the landing. "I suppose I can take my shirt off in front of people who can keep a secret," he says softly, his breath warm against the back of my neck. "Can you keep a secret, Mia?"

I spin around to face him. "Uh, sure. Secrets. Great at them."

"Good to hear. Is that why you're trying to unbutton my shirt?"

"Huh?"

"Your hands," he says simply.

Somehow, my hands are pressed against his chest, my fingers toying with the buttons on his crisp, white shirt. The crisp, white shirt covering a hard, muscular chest. A chest that would look amazing with a tattoo on it . . . Whoa. What is going on here? Why am I thinking about Pierre's chest? Why am I thinking about tattoos on his chest?

I pull my hands away. "Um, I gotta go. I forgot something at the doctor's office."

As I dart up the stairs, Pierre calls out, "I'll catch you later, okay? I still want to get your opinion on that tattoo."

I mutter something non-committal, continuing to run up the stairs. Isabelle would be proud of the pace I'm setting.

When I reach the next level, I slump on the floor and put my head in my hands. Then I cringe. My hands are covered in sweat. Me, of all people, with gross, sweaty hands. I groan as I grapple with two horrifying questions— Did I leave sweat prints all over Pierre's shirt? And what is it about this guy that caused me to break out into a nervous sweat?

CHAPTER 3
CORNETTOS VS. CROISSANTS

A week later, Isabelle and I are sipping cappuccinos in Italy. This was not the original plan, as Isabelle likes to remind me.

When the cruise ship docked in near Rome, we had planned to make our way directly to Germany. But we had been having so much fun with Ginny on the transatlantic crossing to Europe, I suggested that we join her in Ravenna, a quaint city near the Adriatic Sea. While Ginny was in cooking school during the day, Isabelle and I could explore the city. Then, in the evenings, we'd all hang out and eat delicious Italian food.

After a quick search online, I snagged a last-minute deal on an adorable vacation rental in the heart of the city, and we hopped on the train with Ginny. Now here we are, sitting in a picturesque courtyard, surrounded by terracotta planters overflowing with flowers, and listening to the sound of water bubbling in a marble fountain.

"Admit it," I say to Isabelle. "Spending a week in Italy was a great idea of mine."

She furrows her brow. "Well, I suppose."

"You're just upset because you didn't have time to do hours and hours of extensive research, make a detailed itinerary, and—"

Isabelle holds up her hand. "There's nothing wrong with being organized."

"There's organized, then there's *organized.* No wonder you loved being in the Air Force so much. All that structure. You knew exactly what you were supposed to do every minute of the day." I shudder. "I couldn't have ever handled it."

Isabelle laughs so hard, she almost snorts coffee out of her nose. "No kidding. You wouldn't have lasted a minute in the military." Then her face grows serious. "Actually, that's one of the things I love about you—you're so impetuous."

"Impetuous?" I ask. "Is that one of your Scrabble words?"

"You have *Star Wars.* I have Scrabble," she says with a smile.

I shrug. "I guess they both start with the letter 'S.'"

"You know what I mean. You're carefree. You make decisions on the spur of the moment. You're not afraid to try new things."

I squeeze her hand. "You're perfect as you are. And besides, we make a good team."

"Yeah, kind of like *The Odd Couple*."

"Which one was that one again?"

"We just saw it on the cruise ship. How is it that you can only remember movies that have Bruce Willis in them or are part of the *Star Wars* franchise?" Isabelle rolls her eyes. "It was the one starring Jack Lemmon and Walter Matthau as Felix and Oscar. You're Oscar, the fun-loving slob—"

"Oh, yeah, I remember now. You're Felix, the neurotic control freak."

"I don't know about freak," she says with a smile. Then her expression sobers. "I'm going to miss you."

"I'm going to miss you too, but you'll meet lots of fun people at your new job."

She fidgets with her bracelet. "You know how much I hate meeting new people. I get so shy."

"But you did great making friends with

Ginny and Celeste on the cruise. In fact, you were the one who introduced yourself to Ginny."

"That was hard, but I'm trying to force myself out of my comfort zone. Working with my new therapist has made me realize that I need to take more chances." She gulps. "But I may have gone too far accepting this job in Germany."

Before I can reassure her that everything is going to be okay, a baritone voice behind me says, "*Buongiorno, signore.*"

I turn and see Lorenzo, the owner of the apartment we're renting. He sets a pastry box on the wrought-iron table, then leans down and greets us European-style with kisses on our cheeks.

"I brought some Italian delicacies for you to try." He looks around the courtyard. "Where is your *bellissimo* friend, Ginny?"

"She's at her cooking class," Isabelle says.

Lorenzo's shoulders slump. "That is a shame."

"But she'll be back here tonight," Isabelle says. "She's going to meet us for dinner."

His face brightens. "Good. Perhaps I will see her then."

I smile, wondering if I should warn Ginny that Lorenzo has the hots for her. First, there was that American guy on the train who kept flirting with her. Now there's this Italian dude who appears to be after her.

"Try one of these," Lorenzo says, placing a crescent-shaped pastry in front of me.

"It looks like a croissant."

"A croissant?" The horrified expression on his face reminds me of the look on my mother's face when I came home from high school one day with a purple mohawk. "Croissants are

French . . . how do you say it . . . they are *ripugnante.*"

Even though I don't speak Italian, I can tell that *ripugnante* is not something one should aspire to be. Especially if one is a pastry.

Lorenzo continues, "This is a *cornetto.* It means 'little horn' in English. Try it. It is delicious. Far superior to a croissant."

Isabelle takes a delicate bite of hers and murmurs appreciatively. I take a much larger bite, and groan with pleasure. Inside the soft, eggy dough is a rich custard cream. I quickly devour the rest of it.

Lorenzo smiles and hands me another one. "It is good to see a woman that has a healthy appetite."

My phone buzzes. As I lick cream off my fingers and reach for it, Isabelle says, "Is that Pierre again?"

"What do you mean *again*?"

"He's texted you a million times since we got off the cruise ship."

"That's a bit of an exaggeration," I say.

"Really. Count them up for me. I'll bet there's at least a hundred."

"Sure, but you're going to lose." Scrolling through my texts, I lose count after the thirtieth. "Okay, maybe there were a few from him," I admit.

"Who is Pierre?" Lorenzo asks. "That is a French name."

"He's Mia's boyfriend," Isabelle jokes.

"No, he's not. He's just a friend."

"Good," Lorenzo says. "The French do not understand pastry."

I laugh and take a selfie of myself eating a cornetto. I send it to Pierre along with the message, *Cornettos – 1, Croissants – 0.*

He responds immediately. *You need to get out of Italy. They're brainwashing you with inferior pastries.*

They don't taste inferior to me.

That's the brainwashing talking. Come to France so we can deprogram you.

But these have cream inside.

Wait until you try our pain au chocolat. Croissants filled with chocolate.

I smile mischievously as I type my reply. *I don't like chocolate.*

WHAT? I thought all girls liked chocolate.

But I'm not like other girls.

He sends a GIF of Princess Leia that says, "She's royalty."

Hardly, I type back. *I'm a commoner.*

There's nothing common about you.

I roll my eyes at his cheesiness, then text him a bunch of cheese emojis.

Are you saying you want a cheese croissant? That can be arranged.

I decide it's time to set the record straight. *Confession: I love chocolate.*

Phew. I don't have to return the box of chocolates I bought you.

You bought me chocolate?

To celebrate.

Celebrate what?

Your new job! Check your email.

I munch on a third cornetto while I

check my inbox. These are delicious. I'm afraid Pierre's croissants are up against some stiff competition. As I read through the email Pierre sent me, I almost drop my pastry in shock.

"Did you just squeal?" Isabelle asks.

"Do I look like a guinea pig?" I say, placing my half-eaten cornetto back in the box. "That was a high-pitched yelp. Completely different from a squeal."

"Sounded like a squeal to me," she says dryly. "What happened?"

"A job at a small art gallery located at a boutique hotel in Paris. Pierre knows the manager." I scroll back through the email. "They're looking for someone who speaks English."

"You speak English."

"Yeah, but there are a million people who speak English. Why would they be interested in me? There has to be something Pierre isn't telling me."

* * *

While Lorenzo tells Isabelle all about *lucha libre*—apparently he has aspirations to move to Mexico and become a huge wrestling star—I stare at my phone, trying to figure out how to respond to Pierre's offer to help me land my dream job.

A large gray cat saunters across the courtyard, then jumps into my lap. He sniffs at my half-eaten cornetto before I pull him back.

"Sorry, bub. That one has my name on it. Not to mention my teeth marks." While I savor the buttery pastry, the cat nestles in my lap, purring loudly. "Pierre is off his rocker. There's no way a croissant can compete with this. So delicious."

After popping the last bit into my mouth, I stroke the cat's fur. "So, what do you think I should do? If I take this job, it would be because some guy helped me, not because I earned it on my own. You remember the last time that happened, don't you?"

The cat rolls over on his side and looks at me quizzically. Then he nudges my hand with his head, indicating exactly where he wants to be scratched.

"Well, of course you don't remember the last time that happened. I just met you." As I scratch behind his ears, I fill him in. "You see, when I worked at the country club, there was this guy. This really rich guy. You know, one of those CEO-types. Some sort of tech start-up . . . or was it an IT firm? Maybe a lingerie company?"

The cat meows sharply, giving me an impatient look, apparently uninterested in how the guy had made his money and more interested in a distraction-free petting.

"Okay, I guess that's not important. Well, anyway, I always wanted to go to art school, but I couldn't afford it. And it's not like my parents were in any position to help out. Just when I thought

I was going to be a waitress for the rest of my life, this guy says that he can get me a scholarship. I couldn't believe my luck."

I pause and check the pastry box to see if there are any more cornettos left. Nope, just boring, dry, crunchy biscotti. I break off a piece and offer it to the cat. He spits it out. I can't say that I blame him. Biscotti definitely don't make my top-ten cookie list. Maybe Italians should stick to making cornettos.

"So, where was I? Oh, yeah, the rich dude and his scholarship. You'd think I would have learned my lesson the first time I got involved with a rich guy, but I didn't. He suggested that I come to his house for drinks so that he could help me fill out the application. I assumed his wife would be there. She wasn't. And you can imagine what happened next. He expected something in return for his generous offer. I told him where he could shove it. The next day when I showed up to work at the country club, the manager pulled me aside and told me one of the members had filed a complaint against me and that they had to let me go. You seem like a smart kitty. I bet you can guess who that was."

Isabelle glances at me. "Are you talking to yourself again?"

"No, I'm talking to the cat," I say. "He's a good listener."

"His name is Bacio," Lorenzo says.

"Can you hand me a napkin?" I ask. "He's drooling."

"That means he is happy," Lorenzo says. "What were you telling him? It must be a good story."

"Not so much a good story as an age-old story," I say. "Rich guy offers to help, but the offer comes with strings."

"That is what this Pierre is?" Lorenzo asks. "A rich guy with stringy job offer?"

I laugh, thinking this is probably what it sounds like when I speak French. "Not stringy job offer. Job offer with strings."

Lorenzo furrows his brow. "Strings? Like a violin?"

"It doesn't matter," Isabelle says. "Pierre isn't rich. He's a waiter. There aren't any strings."

"Actually, he was a waiter," I say. "Now he's a bellboy."

"Really? When did that happen?" she asks.

"It just happened. His contract with the cruise ship ended, and he got a job at the hotel where the art gallery is located."

"Honestly, I don't see what the big deal is. Pierre is just a nice guy trying to help you out. So what if he knows the manager? That's probably how he got his job too. It's just good luck, that's all."

"You're the one with good luck," I tell her. "After all, you won the tickets for our transatlantic cruise. But when it comes to me, there's no such thing as good luck. Only bad luck initially disguised as good luck."

Lorenzo gives me a bemused look as he pulls his long hair back into a ponytail. "Ah, I understand now."

"You mean the string thing?" I ask.

"No. I understand why you hesitate to accept the job offer. You have romantic feelings for this Pierre."

I scoff. "Pierre? Romantic feelings? Hardly."

"I see it in your eyes. Italian men have romantic sixth sense."

I fold my arms across my chest. "I think your romance sensor is broken. The only feelings I have for Pierre are as a friend."

Lorenzo considers my response. After a few moments, he shrugs. "Okay. Then I set you up with my cousin. He also wants to be a *lucha libre* wrestler."

CHAPTER 4
GRAMMATICAL CONFUSION

Okay, I ended up saying yes. Not to Lorenzo's offer to set me up with his cousin—a wrestler wearing spandex, a cape, and a mask isn't really my idea of a dream guy—but to Pierre. Maybe Isabelle is right. Maybe my luck has changed for the better. I'd be a fool not to take him up on his offer to help me get a job at a Parisian art gallery. He doesn't have a hidden agenda. He's just an ordinary guy looking to help out a friend.

Although, if I'm honest, my bank account helped make the decision for me. Whenever I log on to check my balance, there's a lot of red on the screen. At first, I thought it was some sort of decorative thing for the holidays, like a Rudolph the Reindeer or candy-cane themed web design.

Isabelle put a damper on that idea, pointing out that: (a) Christmas is a long way off; (b) banks aren't known for taking a festive approach to accounting; and (c) at the rate I'm spending money, I'd be lucky to be able to afford a candy cane.

She explained to me that red is bad and black is good. That only made sense to me after she pointed out that, when it comes to clothes, black is slimming. Looking slimmer is good. Therefore, numbers that are black are good. Then she helped me put together a budget. When we got done, I realized how much I needed a paying job. And that's when I sent a text to Pierre saying, "*Oui.*"

He sent back a picture of a flaky croissant and a link to a timer counting down the days until I arrive in France and try the best pastry the world has ever known.

Finally, the moment has come. After traveling around Europe for a few weeks, I'm at Gare de Lyon in the heart of Paris, stepping off the overnight train from Italy. I sling my *Star Wars* backpack over my shoulder and wheel my suitcase toward the end of the platform.

My breath catches when I glimpse Pierre standing on the other side of the ticket barrier holding a bouquet of flowers. The color seems odd—they have kind of a brownish hue to them—but maybe wilted flowers were all that he could afford on a bellboy's salary. It's the thought that counts, right?

As I elbow my way through the throng

of travelers, I chew on my lip. Why did Pierre get me flowers? That's not something you normally do for someone you're just friends with. Maybe it's a Parisian thing, like eating snails.

Once I pass through the barrier, Pierre saunters toward me. No lazy grin this time. The man is full on beaming at me. For some reason, I can't move my feet. They're stuck to the tiled floor. I must have stepped in some bubblegum. A rather large wad of incredibly sticky bubblegum because no matter how much I will my feet to walk in Pierre's direction, they refuse to obey.

When Mr. Hazel Eyes reaches me, he cups my face with one hand and plants a soft, lingering kiss on my cheek. Then he slowly turns my head and kisses the other cheek. I'm used to these European-style kisses from my time in Italy, but this seems different. Really different. Instead of the casual "hello" vibe I usually get when someone greets me, these kisses seem to promise something more.

I take a deep breath, inhaling the scent of his cologne. It's a blend of sandalwood, bergamot, and something else I can't quite put my finger on. Wait a minute. Is that bread I'm smelling?

I glance down at the bouquet of flowers, except they're not flowers— they're croissants, each one fastened on a "stem" made out of a green bamboo skewer adorned with paper leaves. I burst out laughing. I love this guy's sense of humor. And this totally makes sense now. You get a girl that you're just friends with a bouquet of pastries, not flowers.

"*Bienvenue en France*," Pierre says softly, in a silky French accent. It reminds me of the rich chocolate mousse filling you find in a French silk pie. It's my mom's go-to dessert when the ladies from church come over for lunch. It's a time-consuming recipe, but so worth it. Although, I'm pretty sure there's nothing French about it since the pie crust she uses is made from Oreo cookies. But the ladies sure do drool over it.

While I'm surreptitiously wiping drool from the corner of my mouth—just thinking about my mom's pie will cause that to happen—Pierre switches to English. His British accent reminds me of crème brûlée. There's a smoothness to it that evokes the creamy, vanilla-flavored custard base, but there's also a crisp overtone, like crunchy burnt caramel topping which is the hallmark of crème brûlée.

I can't decide which accent I prefer. Come to think of it, I can't decide which dessert I prefer either.

"I hope you're hungry," Pierre says. "My friend at the bakery made these especially for you."

"Really? That was sweet. I don't even know him."

"Her," Pierre clarifies.

"Her?" I ask, my voice cracking slightly.

The corners of his mouth twitch. "Yes, her. *Elle*. I have female friends. Does that bother you?"

"Of course not. I'm female, and we're friends." I gesture at the bouquet. "That's a lot of croissants."

"One for each day you were in Italy eating those awful cornettos."

"I count more than seven."

"Maths never was my strong suit."

I smile at his British use of *maths* rather than the American *math.* I have to confess that it sounds sexy. His accent, not any reference to mathematics. Math is definitely not sexy. All that addition and subtraction. No wonder my bank account is looking so bleak.

"I wasn't great at math either," I say. "I barely passed algebra in high school."

"How did your parents react?"

"Well, I didn't flunk."

"And that was enough for them?"

"Sure. They had other things to worry about."

"Like what?"

"You know, the usual—paying the mortgage, making sure there was food on the table, that kind of thing."

Pierre looks off into the distance. "People shouldn't have to worry about that kind of thing."

"No, they shouldn't. But when your dad gets laid off, well . . ." My voice trails off as I think about how hard my parents worked to take care of our family. I take a deep breath, then exhale slowly. "But enough about that. Let's talk pastries. The smell of these is driving me crazy."

"If you think the smell is good, wait until you try them." Pierre tears a piece off one of the croissants. I reach my hand up to take the morsel from him, but he pops it in my mouth before I have a chance. He watches me intently as I chew, waiting for my verdict. "Well?"

"Well what?" I ask innocently.

"Did you like the croissant?"

I brush flakes of buttery pastry off my shirt. "It's okay."

He reacts with mock horror. "Okay? Just okay? What did they do to your taste buds in Italy?"

"The food was delicious in Italy— zuppa di pesche, ravioli, bombolones, and, of course, the cornettos were to die for."

Pierre narrows his eyes as I smack my fingers to my lips. He selects another croissant from the bouquet. Instead of tearing off a small piece for me to sample, he presents it to me as if it is a single, exquisite rose. "Try this one. It's a pain au chocolat."

"Ooh, a chocolate croissant," I say.

"Exactly. If you don't fall in love with French pastries after eating this one, well, then, I'll just have you deported."

"Yeah, right," I scoff. "Like a bellboy

has so much pull with the government."

He grins. "Never underestimate bellboys."

After I take a bite of the chocolate croissant, I groan with pleasure. There's no way I can keep up this pretense that French croissants are mediocre. "This is absolutely delicious."

Pierre brushes my lips lightly, wiping off a morsel of chocolate and popping it into his mouth. *"Oui, elle est délicieuse."*

I simultaneously shiver and furrow my brow. A weird physical reaction. But what just happened was weird. The shiver I can write off as some sort of sugar high reaction to the chocolate filling, certainly not Pierre's touch.

The furrowed brow, on the other hand…that's because I'm utterly confused by what he said.

See, here's the problem with the French language—instead of "it" like we use in English, they use masculine and feminine pronouns. *Il* for masculine and *elle* for feminine. So, if we were talking about how a croissant tastes, we'd say, "It is delicious." The French would say, "*Il est délicieux*," using *il* instead of *elle* because croissants are masculine.

But I could swear Pierre said, "*Elle est délicieuse*." There was a whole ton of feminine going on in that sentence—the feminine pronoun, *elle*, and the feminine ending to the word 'delicious.'

There are four explanations that I can think of. Number one is that I didn't pay enough attention in French class, and croissants are feminine after all. That's actually a pretty plausible theory, considering my grades in high school. The second explanation is I misheard Pierre, and he really said, "*It est délicieux*." Also pretty plausible. I was distracted at the time by his fingers brushing against my lips. The third possibility is that Pierre made a mistake, confusing *elle* with *il*. Not very likely, though. He was born and raised in

Paris.

I take another bite of the chocolate croissant, pondering the final explanation. Is it possible that Pierre wasn't talking about the croissant, but instead was talking about me? Was he saying that *she* is delicious? *She* meaning me? Does he think I'm delicious?

No, I tell myself firmly. That is the *least* likely explanation. People don't describe other people as delicious. That's just weird. Sure, I can see that gooey-eyed couple from the cruise ship —the ones who couldn't keep their hands to themselves in public—calling each other delicious, but normal people don't say things like that.

I shake my head. What was I thinking? Pierre would never be interested in me in that way. Polishing off the rest of the croissant, I make a vow to brush up on my French. The last thing I need is a grammatical mishap with Pierre, especially a grammatical mishap of the romantic kind.

* * *

I clutch my half-eaten croissant bouquet while Pierre and I wait at the taxi stand outside the train station.

"First stop, your apartment to drop off the luggage," he says. "Then, I thought we'd swing by the Louvre before I take you to the hotel to meet your new boss."

At the mention of the world's largest art gallery, I clap my hands together in glee, inadvertently squashing a few of the pastries in the process. "I have wanted to go to the Louvre ever since I was seven years old."

"Don't most seven-year-old girls want to have tea parties with their dolls instead of going to museums?"

"I didn't have dolls," I say archly. "I had stuffed animals."

"Is there a difference?"

"A big difference," I say as we get into the taxi.

As we drive toward the *quatrieme arrondissement*, the area in Paris where the apartment I've rented is located, I tell Pierre about my second-grade teacher. "Mrs. Murphy loved art and wanted her students to appreciate it as well. She would show us pictures of famous paintings and ask us what we thought. I fell in love with *The Lacemaker* by the Dutch artist, Johannes Vermeer. I was blown away by the detail, especially on the yellow shawl the lacemaker is wearing. Then Mrs. Murphy told me about this magical place in France—the Louvre—full of even more amazing artwork. That's when I decided that one day I would find a way to get to Paris and see it for myself."

"Well, we only have time for a quick visit today," Pierre says. "But I have a friend who works at the Louvre who can arrange for a private tour at a later date."

"You seem to have a lot of connections. The friend at the bakery, the manager of the art gallery who agreed to hire me sight unseen, your friend at the Louvre—"

Pierre interrupts as we turn down a dark alley. "Are you sure you have the correct address?"

I check my email. "Yep, this is the right street."

The taxi comes to a halt in front of a dilapidated building. The exterior brickwork is cracked in a way that would probably make a structural engineer nervous. The front door is hanging off the hinges. Most of the windows are boarded up. Those that aren't have cracked window panes, which I suppose are good for ventilation. I hear it gets hot in Paris during the summer.

I open the taxi door, but before I can get out, Pierre pulls me back in. "You can't possibly be serious about staying here."

"I'm sure it's fine inside," I say. "The landlord did warn me that they were doing renovations to the building. That's why the rent is so cheap."

As I scoot out of the taxi, I hear Pierre telling the driver to wait for us. When I try to open the trunk to get my bag, Pierre puts his hand on top of mine and shakes his head. "No, you're not staying here."

I snatch my hand away. "Of course I am. Do you know how hard it is to find an apartment in Paris that I can afford? Do you expect me to sleep on the street?"

"The street would be better than this place."

I spin around and flounce up the stairs, avoiding the piles of garbage in my path. When I try to pull the front door open, it won't budge. Pierre comes up behind me and yanks forcefully on the handle, his biceps bulging underneath his t-shirt. The door pulls free from the hinges, and Pierre sets it to the side.

"After you, my lady," he says, bowing at the waist.

I cautiously walk inside, gagging at the stench, which I suspect is coming from the black mold peeking out from behind the peeling wallpaper.

Pierre looks at me, his hazel eyes steely. "Seen enough?"

"No. I haven't seen my apartment yet. It's on the fourth floor. They're probably doing renovations from the top floor downward." I dash up the stairs, calling out behind me. "Come on. I bet you twenty euros that it's really charming."

By the time I make it to my floor, I'm gasping for breath. I had forgotten that the French number their floors differently. What we call the first floor, they call the ground floor. Our second floor is their first floor, and so on. So when I got to what I thought was the fourth floor, it turns out it was only the third floor. It was a struggle to climb that final set of stairs, let me tell you.

When we reach my apartment, Pierre pokes his head inside. "This is charming?"

"Well, at least I don't need your help to open the door."

"That's because there isn't a door," he says dryly.

"Technicalities," I say, following him into the main living area.

"There aren't any windows either. Is that another one of your technicalities?" Pierre folds his arms across his chest. "This is definitely not *charmant*."

Before I can argue with him, a rat scurries across the floor and stops in front of me. He raises himself on his hind legs, sniffs the air, then starts to climb up my jeans. I scream and drop my bouquet. Fortunately, the rat jumps off my leg. Unfortunately, he begins feasting on one of the almond filled croissants.

"Tell you what," Pierre says. "You can forget about the twenty euros you owe me if you agree that you're not going to stay here."

"Agreed. But where am I going to stay?" I put my head in my hands.

He pulls his phone out of his pocket. "Don't worry about it. I'll take care of it."

By the time we're back at the taxi, he's arranged accommodations for me. "It's perfect for you. No commute to work."

"What do you mean 'no commute'?"

"I got you a room at the Hôtel de la Marmotte."

I gulp. Hôtel de la Marmotte is where the art gallery I'm going to be working at is located. It's also one of the trendiest hotels in Paris. "There's no way I can afford that."

"The concierge is a buddy of mine. He's arranged for you to stay in it for free for as long as you need. It's a spare room that the hotel normally keeps vacant." Pierre puts his arm around my shoulders and gives me a squeeze. "It's all taken care of. I'll have the taxi drop off your luggage at the hotel and you and I can walk to the Louvre."

My jaw tightens. Pierre is starting to sound like my ex-husband. Swooping in and saving the damsel in distress. Taking care of things. Calling in favors from his buddies for the little woman. I want so desperately to refuse Pierre's offer, but what choice do I have? Finding another apartment is going to take some time. I'm too exhausted from the train ride to tackle that now. And, besides, the Louvre awaits.

* * *

"I can't believe I finally got to see the *Mona Lisa*," I say to Pierre as we leave the Louvre. Pausing to take a picture of the glass pyramid structure that towers over the museum courtyard, I try to decide whether I like the juxtaposition of I.M. Pei's modern design with the classic French Renaissance architecture of the original building.

I decide that I do like it. In a way it's like what I do—taking classic oil paintings and transforming them into something new using tattoo needles and ink.

"Did you have any other favorites?" Pierre asks as he hails a taxi.

"Oh, yes. The one by Georges le Tour."

"Which one was that again?"

"*The Card Sharp with the Ace of Diamonds*," I say. "It was the one depicting a card game."

"Oh, yeah. That poor guy. Oblivious to the fact that he's being cheated."

"Serves him right, don't you think? Wealthy people think they're so entitled. It's nice to see them get their comeuppance, even if it's only in an oil painting from the 1600s."

Pierre furrows his brow. "That's not really what you think about rich people, is it?"

"Maybe they're not all like that," I concede.

Pierre is quiet during the ride to the hotel. Occasionally, he points out landmarks, like the Jardin des Tuilieres and the Place de la Concorde, but for the most part, he stares at his phone, a pained expression in his eyes. I wonder if it's a touch of indigestion. We did eat a lot of the croissants before I sacrificed the rest of the bouquet to the rat.

"We're here," he announces. "Notice the panes in the windows and the absence of rodents?"

"Ha-ha." I've come to terms with staying at this luxury hotel while I look for another apartment to rent. Sure, I don't like that Pierre had to come to my rescue, and he probably could have done with less of a take-charge attitude, but he's a nice guy who's just trying to come to my aid.

As one of the bellboys opens the door and helps me out of the taxi, I stifle a laugh. I can't picture Pierre wearing this get-up—a red, double-breasted fitted jacket with a band collar, gold trim, and way too many buttons, paired with a matching pillbox hat. It looks like something an organ grinder's monkey would wear, not a grown man.

Pierre and the bellboy joke around with each other for a few moments while I stare in awe at the ornate marble facade of the hotel. This place is so fancy that even the members of the country club back home might feel uncomfortable here.

A woman wearing a gray suit rushes out. "Pierre, *la directrice de l'hôtel aimerait te voir. Bouge-toi.*"

I give him a sideways glance. "Hmm . . . The director of the hotel wants to see you. That can't be good."

He sighs. "No. I can't imagine it is."

"Don't worry," I say. "Just be your usual charming self and sweet talk her."

He gives me a wry smile, then places his hand on the small of my back and ushers me into the lobby. "Jean-Paul, can you look after Mia while I take care of something?"

A distinguished-looking older man comes round from the concierge's desk, takes my hand in his and kisses the back of it. "It would be my pleasure."

"Jean-Paul, you smooth talker, you." Pierre pulls my hand away and cups it between his. I smile at the reference to that cute scene in *The Empire Strikes Back* where Lando Calrissian flirts with Princess Leia. "Save it for your wife."

Jean-Paul holds his hands up. "Ah, do not worry. My wife is the only woman I have eyes for."

"How long have you been married?" I ask.

"Almost thirty-five years." Jean-Paul beams as he tells me how he met his wife.

The woman in the gray suit waves urgently at Pierre.

"I have to go," Pierre says to me. "Jean-Paul is the head concierge at Hôtel de la Marmotte. Any questions you have about the hotel or Paris, he can help you with."

"Go, go," Jean-Paul says. "I'll get Mia settled in her accommodations, then introduce her to Amélie."

"Amélie is the manager of the art gallery and Jean-Paul's wife," Pierre explains before he rushes off.

Jean-Paul chuckles. "It's good to have him back in Paris. I've known him since he was a baby. He's grown into a fine young man."

"Ooh, I bet you have some great stories about him as a kid."

"I certainly do. And for the right price, I'll tell you, especially the embarrassing ones." Jean-Paul hands me his business card. "Now, first things first.

These are my contact details. If you need anything at all, let me know."

"Thanks, that's really sweet." I inspect the card, smiling at the hotel's quirky logo of a yellow-bellied marmot sitting in a claw-foot bathtub. I love that they've named this hotel after an adorable furry rodent. The place might be fancy, but it also has a sense of humor.

Then I frown when I read the small print underneath the hotel's name—a Toussaint property.

"Toussaint," I muse. "That's Pierre's last name."

Jean-Paul cocks his head to one side. "Yes, that's correct. Pierre Toussaint."

I chuckle. "For a minute there, I thought he was related to the owners of this hotel, but I guess it's a pretty common name."

"But he *is* related to the owners. They are his parents. Didn't you know? Pierre is the heir to the Toussaint fortune."

CHAPTER 5
LOVE IS LIKE A TOOTHACHE

"The Toussaint fortune?" I splutter. "What are you telling me? Pierre is some sort of billionaire?"

Jean-Paul smiles. "I have no idea what his net worth is. It's not something we discuss. We talk about more important things like the rugby."

"Pierre plays rugby?" I've always been fascinated by rugby. Men in striped jerseys and shorts engaged in a full contact sport, which is similar in some ways to American football, but without the protective gear.

"He did when he was in college, but then he was injured."

Rugby explains a lot. His confidence, which borders on cockiness at times. His slightly misshapen left ear. His broad shoulders. His muscular chest. His—

Whoa. I need to stop this train of thought. Get your mind out of the gutter, Mia. Remember who Pierre is—a rich, pretentious guy who likes to dole out favors so that you'll bow down and worship him. He is not someone who you should fantasize about. Focus.

"So, Jean-Paul, tell me about Pierre's injury. What happened?" There, that should be a safe topic. Injured guys are so unsexy.

Jean-Paul's face clouds over. "That's something you should probably ask him about."

"Okay . . . well maybe you can answer this. If he's so rich, why is he working as a bellboy? Shouldn't he be wearing a suit and tie, sitting in some fancy boardroom, sipping on scotch and counting his money?"

"Pierre wants to learn all aspects of the hotel business. It's important to him to have hands-on experience. Earlier this year, he worked as a receptionist at the front desk. Before that, he was a dishwasher in the kitchen. After his rotation as a bellboy, he's going to work for me as an assistant concierge."

"Won't that be strange—you being the boss of the, well, the, um, boss?"

"Pierre has a . . . what do you call it . . . he has an egalitarian spirit. He thinks everyone is equal."

I guess I can see how people might think that. Pierre was joking around with the bellboys earlier, and the woman from the front desk spoke to him informally, telling him to hurry up. But at the end of the day, the boss is the boss.

"And don't forget. I've known Pierre

since he was a baby. I've even changed his diapers. He knows who's boss."

Jean-Paul chuckles. It's infectious—a mixture of Santa Claus-style ho-ho-hos and Mr. Rogers' more sedate laughter. I find myself joining in, my grin turning to full-fledged belly laughs as I picture Pierre in a baby-sized rugby jersey and diapers.

When I catch my breath, I ask about Pierre's stint as a waiter. "Does his family own the cruise ship?"

"No, they are strictly hoteliers. The cruise ship line is owned by friends of the family. Rather than work at one of the hotel restaurants, Pierre thought it would be a good idea to get experience as a waiter elsewhere because . . ." Jean-Paul's voice trails off. He gives me a penetrating gaze, then stares at the floor. "Perhaps you should ask—"

"Ask Pierre? Got it."

Jean-Paul looks back up at me. "We're all delighted that he's back now.

He seems so happy since he returned. I think you have something to do with that."

"Me?"

He grins. "Yes, you. In fact, I haven't seen him this happy since he came back from Africa."

I shake my head. "Africa?"

"Hasn't he told you about his time in Africa?"

"No," I say slowly. Now that I think about it, Pierre hasn't told me much about himself. All we seem to talk about is *Star Wars*, croissants, and tattoos. "What was he doing in Africa?"

Not surprisingly, Jean-Paul gives me an evasive answer.

"Never mind," I say. "I get it. It's something I should ask Pierre about."

"That would be best," the older man says. "Now, why don't I show you to your room? You can freshen up before you meet Amélie."

As Jean-Paul leads the way to the

elevator, I ponder our conversation. In a short space of time, I've discovered there's a lot I didn't know about Pierre. He's loaded. He has a mysterious injury. He's spent time in Africa. And, for some reason, he didn't want to work as a waiter at one of his family's hotels.

What other secrets is he hiding from me?

* * *

Jean-Paul inserts the key card and opens the door to my new accommodations. After he carries my suitcase in for me, I walk into the room, my feet sinking into the plush oriental carpet.

As I set my *Star Wars* backpack on a carved wooden console table, I check out my surroundings. Oddly, there's no bed. Just living room furniture. But this isn't the kind of furniture you'd find in your average American's home. No, there is some seriously fancy stuff going on here. A large bay window is flanked by a Louis the Sixteenth settee and armchairs . . . or is that Louis the Fifteenth? Why all these old rich dudes all had to have the same name is beyond me. Anyway, the point is that this is the type of stuff royalty would sit primly on while sipping sherry or whatever it is that people drank back then, not a sectional couch from Ikea that a dude named Lou would lounge on in his boxer shorts munching on a bag of potato chips.

What really perplexes me is figuring out where I'm supposed to sleep. I'm pretty sure the settee isn't hiding a foldaway bed inside its silk, toile upholstery fabric. I turn to ask Jean-Paul about it, but he's disappeared. I peek behind the heavy brocade curtains, but he's not hiding there. He isn't on the balcony either, or behind the potted plants.

Okay, I really doubt that a distinguished-looking Parisian concierge is playing hide and seek, but it does give me a good opportunity to have a nosy.

As I'm looking in the closet, I hear someone clear their throat. Jean-Paul is standing in a doorway that I assume leads to the bathroom.

"Is everything to your satisfaction?"

"Yeah, it's great," I say.

"If you'll let me know which bedroom you prefer, I'll place your suitcase in there."

"Which bedroom? You mean there's more than one?"

"Yes," Jean-Paul says nonchalantly. "They're back this way, across from the kitchen and dining room."

I rub my temples. "Kitchen, dining room, bedrooms . . . this isn't a simple hotel room, is it?"

"Well, this is a bit simpler than some of our suites. It doesn't have a humidor or sauna."

"Considering I don't smoke cigars or like to sweat, I think I can live with that."

Jean-Paul smiles kindly at me, and I instantly regret my sarcastic tone.

"I'm sorry, it's just that this is really overwhelming. When Pierre offered me the spare hotel room to stay in temporarily, I envisioned a converted broom closet."

"You're probably tired from your trip. You took the overnight train from Italy, right? Why don't you rest for a while? I'll arrange for you to meet Amélie later." Jean-Paul looks at his watch. "Shall we say two hours from now?"

A nap does sound good. I pick the bedroom that's decorated in subdued blue tones. The only pop of color is a large oil painting of a marmot hanging above the fireplace. It makes me smile. A painting of a marmot wearing a Scottish kilt and tam isn't exactly something you expect to find in a fancy hotel suite. But that's what this place is known for—its quirky touches.

I lie down on the four-poster bed and exhale slowly. What am I going to do? I can't in good conscience stay here. Rolling over on my side, I press my face into the soft down pillow. Again, not the type of pillow you'd buy at Ikea. This thing is probably stuffed with phoenix feathers. And, yes, I know that phoenixes are mythical creatures. But, if you're wealthy, you can probably employ a team of geneticists to create your very own phoenix in a lab, just so you can pluck its feathers for your pillows.

The phoenix pillows do their job, and I feel myself drifting off to sleep. An hour later, the alarm on my phone jolts me awake. There's nothing worse than waking up abruptly when you're having a weird dream. And a dream of Pierre playing rugby while dressed in a marmot costume is pretty weird.

While I take a bath—complete with begonia-scented bubbles and rubber duckies—I consider my options. Stay at the hotel and take the art gallery job or move into the boarded-up, rat-infested apartment and try to find another paying gig.

After toweling off and getting dressed, I make up my mind. Rats and unemployment it is.

"Why do you have your suitcase?" Jean-Paul asks when I walk up to the concierge desk.

Before I can answer, a middle-aged man wearing a business suit steps in front of me and brusquely asks Jean-Paul to organize a skydiving excursion near Paris. I feel a shudder course through my body. I've had to fly a few times when car, train, or bus travel wasn't an option, but it's always involved a panic attack that not even a giant-size Toblerone chocolate bar can cure. Voluntarily getting into a plane, then choosing to jump out of it? Wow, talk about insane.

Jean-Paul asks one of the other concierges to escort me to the art gallery while he assists the businessman with his high altitude death wish.

The Galérie d'Art Animalier is located on the ground floor of the hotel. When the concierge leads me through an entrance off of the lobby, I immediately understand why the gallery has the name it does. Everywhere I look are paintings, photographs, and sculptures of various animals. The styles range from serious to whimsical. Something for every animal lover, regardless of their stylistic preferences.

I spot a woman lightly running a feather duster over a picture frame. Everything about her screams elegance. Her makeup is flawless, her silver hair is pulled back in a classic chignon, and her tailored suit looks like it came from a chic boutique. When she sees us, she sets the duster down, then gracefully walks over to us.

After the concierge makes the introductions, Amélie kisses me on each cheek. *"Enchantée."*

I try to dredge up the correct response from my high school French days. *"Ç'est un plaisir faire votre connaissance."*

She waves a perfectly manicured finger at me playfully. "No French, please. I need to practice English. That is one of the reasons I hired you. I would like to improve my English."

"Uh, about that. I don't think I can take the job."

She presses her hand to her chest. "What? No, I am counting on you. Madame Vernier is counting on you. All the ladies are counting on you. Not to mention the dogs. The dogs are counting on you."

I press my fingers underneath my

eyes. "Who exactly are all these people and canines, and why are they counting on me?"

"Didn't Pierre tell you?" When I shake my head, she shrugs. "Ah, perhaps he wanted to surprise you."

"Yes, he's full of surprises," I mutter.

Amélie places her hand on my arm. "I knew you would be perfect for this job when I read your articles on *Art Girl Moderne*."

I'm stunned. *Art Girl Moderne* is an obscure webzine run by a friend of mine. Its readership is small. I mean, really small. You could fit all of them on a sectional couch from Ikea and still have room for Lou and his bag of potato chips. How the manager of a chic art gallery in Paris stumbled across it is beyond me.

"Your take on Rembrandt's brush strokes was . . . what is the word I am looking for?"

"Boring?"

"*Non*, not boring." She smiles at me. "I could tell from the minute I make your *conaissance* that you could never be boring. It was insightful. That is the word —insightful."

Considering I've never been called insightful in my life, I'm still pretty sure that the word she meant was "boring."

"I received your paperwork and a copy of your work visa and everything is in order. Normally, we pay employee salaries in arrears. But, you probably have many expenses settling into a new city." Amélie hands me a pad of paper and a fountain pen. "Write down your account details and I will arrange for an advance to be transferred to your account."

And just like that, I've been bulldozed into accepting the job in the most charming French way.

* * *

"Mia, Mia, are you there? I can't see you."

Celeste is on the other end of the phone, trying out her new video chat app, while I'm walking along the Seine River back to my rat-infested apartment. It's a long walk, especially with luggage in tow, but taking a taxi is out of the question. Even though Amélie is going to give me an advance on my salary, things are still tight financially.

"Turn the phone around. Good, there you go. Now I can see your face. Can you see mine?"

"I can. Don't you look pretty, dear. Paris must be agreeing with you."

"I don't know about that. I've been here less than twelve hours and my life is a mess." I slump down on a bench, being careful to avoid stepping in a pile of dog poop. It reminds me of the guys Ginny was stuck next to on the train from Rome to Bologna. Their overpowering body spray smelled like a cross between dog poop and bubblegum. Not a winning combination.

"A mess?" A crease forms on Celeste's brow. "What happened?"

I shake my head. "Oh, never mind. I'm fine, really."

"Fine is what donkeys are after they've had a carrot. You, young lady, are not fine."

"Donkeys? Carrots?"

"Haven't you ever fed a donkey a carrot?"

I chuckle. "Not that I can remember. Do guinea pigs count?"

"No, dear. Donkeys and guinea pigs are completely different when it comes to carrots."

"They are?"

"Trust me on this one. Anyway, let's get back to what's wrong."

My feet are aching and I could use a break, so I settle back against the bench and fill her in on everything that's happened with Pierre, from the bouquet of croissants he presented me with to discovering he has a secret life.

"You know what George Burns said about love, don't you?"

"Who's George Burns?"

Celeste blinks her eyes rapidly. "Did you just ask who George Burns is? He was only the funniest man in show biz. Sexy too."

"I think you mean Bruce Willis. The perfect combination of deadpan delivery and a receding hairline."

"Bruce who?"

"You know, *Die Hard*."

"Die hard? Why would I want to do that? I'd rather die soft. Like a Tootsie Roll."

I shake my head. "I think we're talking about two different things."

"I was talking about love."

"I thought you were talking about George Burns?"

"I was. Anyway, he said that love is like a toothache. It doesn't show up on x-rays, but you know it's there."

"My teeth feel fine."

"But your heart doesn't. You've grown attached to Pierre. It always hurts when we find out someone isn't who we thought they were. That's what happened to me with . . . never mind."

"Hurt seems a stretch," I say. "He's just a guy."

"He's more than that."

"Okay, I'll admit it. I thought he was my friend. But friends don't deceive each other like that."

"Did he tell you he was poor?"

"Well, no, not exactly in so many words."

"So how did he deceive you?"

"By not being . . . well, who I thought he was."

"How is he different now that you know he has money?"

"He's a stuck-up snob."

"He's the same person, dear. It's just your perception of him that's changed.

Love is about seeing who someone is, despite their outer trappings."

"I'm not in love with him," I scoff. "I'm . . ."

"You're what?"

"I was attracted to him, okay? But that's it. Insta-attraction, but not insta-love. Fortunately, there are a million cute guys in Paris." I scan the area, then turn the phone so that Celeste can see. "Like that one there."

"You mean the mime, dear?"

"No, not him. The man next to him. The one putting something in the trash can."

"I hate to break it to you, but I don't think he's throwing something out. He's going through the garbage. Poor soul, I think he's homeless."

The guy I had been talking about has already walked away, but Celeste is right. There's another man standing by the trash can. I take a closer look and frown. "Oh, I think you're right. He looks like he sleeps on the street. I might end up sleeping on the street too if my apartment doesn't work out."

"But you're not homeless, dear. You have a lovely hotel suite to stay in while you get your feet on the ground. If I can offer some words of wisdom, you've been fortunate enough to have been given some unexpected blessings. Don't let your pride get in the way. Take the job. Take the offer of temporary housing. Then prove everyone wrong. That's something you like doing, right? Proving people wrong?"

After a few more minutes of motherly advice, Celeste hangs up. I've decided she's half-right. I'll keep the job at the art gallery, but staying at the hotel is a step too far.

I scrounge in my backpack to see if I have any loose change. My feet are killing me and I still have a long walk to my apartment. To my surprise, I find a twenty-euro note tucked in a zippered compartment. I have no idea how it got there, but I don't care. It's my lucky day. I can afford a subway ticket and dinner.

As I head toward the Pont Neuf Métro station, I think about my recent spate of good luck. I look down at the money in my hand, then tap the homeless man on the shoulder and hand it to him. Time to pass some of that good luck along. A little more walking won't hurt me.

After what seems like an eternity, I finally arrive at my apartment building. There have been some changes since I was here earlier. Instead of waiting for me inside, the rats are sitting on the stoop like some sort of welcoming committee. I think the price of entry is a croissant. The smell of the garbage has a more nuanced quality to it. "Nuanced" being a polite way of staying that the stench is unbearable. And there's a new front door.

I distract the rats with a roll of breath mints, then try to open the door. But it won't budge. Probably because it's not so much a door as it is a piece of plywood firmly nailed in place. And this time, I don't have Pierre to help me pry it off.

After breaking a fingernail, I notice a sign affixed to the side of the building. My heart sinks when I read it—*bâtiment condamné*.

Swell. The building is condemned, the rats have devoured the breath mints that I was going to have for dinner, and my feet are killing me. But what's even worse is that I'm going to have to swallow my pride and accept Pierre's offer to stay at the hotel.

CHAPTER 6
PASTRY OVERLOAD

It's been a long couple weeks of hide and seek. Pierre keeps looking for me, and I keep hiding. Easier said than done when you work in the same hotel. Fortunately, he's been on the night shift while I've been working days. It also helps that both of us have been crazy busy in our spare time. He's been focused on projects related to the family business, while I've been completely absorbed helping Amélie and Madame Vernier curate an exhibition at the gallery.

I'm pretty excited about the exhibition. It's right up my alley—photographs of animal-inspired tattoos—and what's even better is that all the proceeds are going to be donated to a no-kill dog shelter. Working with the premier tattoo artists in Paris and world-renown photographers has been a dream come true. For the first time in my life, I feel like I'm doing what I'm meant to be doing and, more importantly, that I belong in the art world.

But there's a lot to get done. Everything has to be ready in time for the launch party. It's the perfect excuse for avoiding Pierre. While I had sent him a gracious text thanking him for helping me land the job and finding me a place to stay, I haven't wanted anything else to do with him. Hence, the elaborate game of hide and seek we have going on.

By the time the end of my second week at the art gallery rolls around, I've become a pro at it.

I'm in the back room on Sunday afternoon framing photographs, when I hear a familiar voice ask Amélie, "Is Mia here?" Setting aside the mat board and cutter I'm using, I crouch behind some large canvasses propped up in the corner.

Amélie rats me out. "I think she's in the back, *cheri.*"

I hear him walking toward the rear of the gallery, each of his custom-made leather shoes making a distinctive sound as he traverses the marble floor. Can footsteps be sexy? If so, his certainly are. As his firm, confident, masculine steps near my hiding spot, I inch backward and hold my breath. There are times when being as short as I am comes in handy, like today. Squeezing into tight spots has become a new specialty of mine.

After a few moments, I hear Pierre's footsteps retreating back into the gallery.

"She's not there," he says to Amélie. "Can you let her know I stopped by when you see her? I texted her last night, but she didn't respond."

I continue to stay hidden. Pierre may be trying to outfox me, leaning against the counter in the gallery, waiting patiently for me to reveal myself. After ten minutes, I decide the coast is clear. But before I can emerge from behind the canvases, I hear the sound of a pair of shoes coming into the back room. It's not Pierre. These footsteps are brisk and impatient, with a sharp staccato clicking noise that high heels make.

They're followed by two other sets of footsteps. The first is another set of high heels, but they have a more gentle quality to them. I know this sound— those heels belong to Amélie. The other set is unfamiliar to me.

My legs cramp up as Amélie and the other woman discuss a display of textile art. Apparently, it's not up to the standards that this other woman expects. Amélie handles the criticism gracefully. If I was in her place, I would have bopped the other lady in the nose by now.

But as their conversation progresses, I realize why Amélie is being so conciliatory. The other woman is *la directrice de l'hôtel*. Generally, it's not a good idea to bop your boss in the nose.

I massage my calf, willing the two of them to stop talking and go on their merry ways. As I reach down to rub my ankle, something licks my hand. Stifling a yelp, I pray that it's not an extraordinarily large rat looking for a croissant. I curl up into a tight ball and close my eyes, but the creature continues to advance toward me, panting heavily in its quest for French pastries.

"Lyonette, *ici*," the hotel director orders.

Lyonette ignores the command, instead pushing its face into mine. That's when I realize, much to my relief, that this isn't a giant rat, it's a poodle.

"Nice doggie," I whisper.

The poodle responds by growling at me. Okay, not such a nice dog after all. As the growls increase in intensity, the poodle shakes, as though it has just had a refreshing swim in the lake. With each shake of its body, the canvasses rock back and forth. I try to stroke the dog to calm it down, but as I place my hand on its fur, it barks loudly and lunges at me. The canvasses crash to the floor, my hiding spot with them.

"Mia, what are you doing down there?" Amélie asks.

I feel my face grow warm as I look up. The director is tapping her foot, her arms folded across her chest. Like Amélie, she has that effortless Parisian chic vibe to her. Her burgundy Chanel suit is accessorized with pearls, and her dark hair is pulled back into an elegant twist.

Lyonette has a similar chic vibe going on with a classic poodle cut, a pearl collar, and burgundy bows on her ears.

"Uh, I dropped something?" I make a show of searching the floor, crawling on my hands and knees and poking under shelves and tables.

"*Assis,*" the *directrice* commands.

So I sit on my haunches. The dog does too.

She smiles approvingly at Lyonette, then frowns at me. Turning to Amélie, she tells her to take care of the problem.

"*Oui, madame,*" Amélie says before following her back out to the main gallery.

I look at the dog, trying to decide which one of us is the problem that needs to be taken care of.

"It's me, isn't it?" I ask Lyonette.

The poodle gives me a haughty look that seems to say, "Duh, of course it's you."

A deep voice with a British accent says, "I don't think she likes you."

I raise my eyes and see Pierre leaning against the door frame, a bemused look on his face. I can't tell whether he's bemused by the ridiculous bellboy uniform he's wearing or by the fact that I'm sitting on the floor trying to interpret dog expressions.

"Who? The dog or the hotel director?"

He laughs. "Possibly both."

Amélie scoots in behind him and helps me to my feet. Then she snaps her fingers and tells Lyonette to go find her mistress. As the dog departs, she gives me a look that says, "So long, loser."

Avoiding eye contact with Pierre, I brush dust off my black high-waisted trousers and smooth down my fuchsia leopard print top. "Oh, well, it's not like it matters since I'm not going to be working here anymore."

Amélie gasps. "You cannot quit."

"I'm not quitting. You're firing me."

"Why would I fire you?"

"Well, I assumed by the way your boss told you to 'take care of the problem' that I didn't have a job here any longer."

Amélie smiles at Pierre. "If people were fired every time they displeased her, there would be no one left working at the hotel. Her bark is worse than her bite."

"Whose bite? The dog's or the director's?"

"Both," Amélie and Pierre say in unison.

"Are you sure?"

"Positive," Amélie says. "Within an hour, she will have forgotten that you were crawling on the floor. What did you drop, by the way?"

"Oh, I don't think she dropped anything," Pierre says. "I think she was hiding from me."

"Why would I hide from you?" I ask.

"I text, I call, but you never respond.

Whenever I come to the gallery to speak to you, you're mysteriously on break. It's obvious. You're avoiding me. And I want to know why."

The last thing I want to do is get into this with Amélie watching us. I run my fingers through my hair. "I'm just busy, that's all."

"No, I don't think that's it." As he shakes his head emphatically, his pillbox hat slides off and rolls toward me.

When I hand it to Pierre, his fingers brush against mine, sending a jolt of electricity through my body. I had forgotten what his touch feels like. It feels good. Real good. Too good.

I step backward, shoving my hands in my pockets. "Yes, it is. I'm super busy with the exhibition. Lots to do."

"Too busy to go to the *Star Wars* convention on Saturday?"

"Tickets sold out months ago." I shrug. "Even if I had the time to go, I couldn't."

"It just so happens that I have tickets."

I lock eyes with him. "You do?"

"Uh-huh. So you'll come?"

Every fiber in my being wants to shout, "Yes!" Not because I want to spend time with Pierre, but because this is the *Star Wars* convention we're talking about. Who in their right mind passes up an opportunity to go to that?

Me, apparently. I hear myself coolly say, "Sorry, but I have to work on Saturday." Amélie starts to contradict me, but I give her a warning look. "Yep, working all next weekend."

"I'll bet you twenty euros, which you still owe me by the way, that I can get you to change your mind," Pierre says.

"Sounds like easy money to me." I straighten my shoulders. This is going to be the easiest twenty euros I've ever made. I'm going to have no problem resisting Pierre.

Then he winks at me, and I suddenly realize this is going to be a lot harder than I thought.

* * *

Pierre's campaign is relentless. Every fifteen minutes, my phone buzzes with a *Star Wars*-related text from him, each ending with a link to the convention website. For the first few hours, I'm mildly amused, but by the time midnight rolls around, I'm over it. I'm wearing out the delete button on my phone, and I've run out of ways to say no.

I finally drift off to sleep, only to be woken at two in the morning with this text: *Roses are red, violets are blue. If you love* Star Wars, *may the Force be with you.*

I send back a GIF of Darth Vader that says, "Don't make me destroy you."

My phone goes silent after that.

I should be relieved. But I'm not.

I should be able to fall peacefully back to sleep. But I don't.

I should be able to stop thinking about Pierre's hazel eyes. But I can't.

All I seem to be able to do is stare at the ceiling, waiting for the sun to rise, wishing I could get the heir to the Toussaint fortune out of my head.

* * *

The next morning, I walk into work, hiding my bleary eyes behind a large pair of sunglasses. Before I put my purse in the back room, I check my phone again. Nope, no more texts from Pierre. I guess my Darth Vader GIF did the trick.

I push my glasses up on my head and sniff the air. Something smells wonderful, and I'm not just talking about the begonia-scented body wash I used in the shower.

"You have an admirer." Amélie sets a large gift basket on the counter.

My stomach growls when I pull back

the red gingham fabric covering the contents. The basket is overflowing with croissants, small jars of raspberry and strawberry preserves, and a crock full of rich, creamy butter.

Amélie points at the card tied to the handle. "Who is it from?"

"It's not signed," I say as I hand it to her.

"Something to Chewbacca on," she reads out loud, then turns to me. "What does this mean?"

"It's a *Star Wars* reference."

"I have never seen this movie. What is a Chewbacca?"

It's way too early in the morning to explain what a Wookie is. I offer her a croissant instead. While Amélie breaks off a piece and delicately spreads butter and jam on it, she asks me why I'm not having one.

"Oh, I'm not hungry," I say, lying through my teeth. But I've accepted enough from Pierre. I'm not going to add more croissants to the list, no matter how delicious they look. I snap a picture of the gift basket and send it to Ginny and Isabelle.

Can you believe the nerve of this guy? Trying to win me over with croissants!

Isabelle responds right away. *The nerve. LOL.* Then she sends me a picture of what she's having for breakfast. *I bet you wouldn't say no to this strudel.*

Depends who gave it to me. If it was from Pierre, then I would have to refuse.

Ginny responds a few minutes later with a historical tidbit. *Did you know that croissants aren't originally French? An Austrian baker, August Zang, introduced the croissant in Paris in 1838. It's an adaptation of an old Austrian pastry, the kipferl, which dates back to the 1300s.*

I file that juicy little morsel away to taunt Pierre with later.

After spending the first part of the morning helping an American couple decide between a stone sculpture by a Zimbabwean artist and an oil painting by an up-and-coming artist from the Bronx —they ended up buying both—I finally break down and devour a croissant. As I'm wiping away telltale crumbs from my blouse, Pierre walks into the gallery. Because he doesn't start his shift until the evening, he's dressed in regular clothes—jeans, a button-down shirt, and sneakers. It's a way better look for him than the organ grinder's monkey costume.

"I see you got my present," he says.

"Oh, was that from you?" I ask innocently. "The card wasn't signed."

"Do you get many pastry baskets from secret admirers?"

I shrug. "Oh, you'd be surprised."

He furrows his brow. "So I have competition?"

"Competition for what?" I ask with all the nonchalance I can muster.

"Not for what. For whom."

Now, I go in for the kill with full-on sarcasm. "For *whom* . . . look at you all fancy with your perfect grammar."

"What would you say?" he asks, his hazel eyes twinkling.

"I'd say for *who.* I'm sure that's wrong, but I didn't have all your advantages in life. How did you get that British accent, anyway? Boarding school?"

His eyes stop twinkling. "Boarding school isn't all it's cracked up to be."

I chew on my lip. There's a story there. Another secret.

But before I can ask him about it, he changes the subject. "So, what time should I pick you up on Saturday?"

I shake my head. "I told you. I can't go. I'm working all weekend."

"That's not what Amélie says."

"Sounds like a misunderstanding. You know how she's trying to improve her English."

"Our conversation was in French." He leans across the counter and plucks a croissant out of the basket. As he tears off a piece, he says, "So, that's settled. You're free to come with me this weekend."

I fold my arms across my chest. This man is infuriating. Always assuming everyone is going to do what he wants, just because he's rich. I refuse to respond. If I stand here long enough, not saying anything, eventually he'll leave, right? Pouty resistance always wins in the end.

Geez, how long does it take to eat a croissant? I want to rip the pastry out of his hand and shove it into his mouth. I want to trace my finger on the side of his mouth and wipe that stray bit of strawberry preserves away. I want to touch his lips. I want to—

Stop it, Mia. Stop thinking about him.

"So, you realize that I'm going to keep sending you croissants until you say yes," Pierre says.

I stamp my foot. "For the love of all

that is flaky, no more croissants."

"Fine. Challenge accepted." He gives me a cocky grin, then walks out of the gallery.

I put my head in my hands and groan. How does he always manage to turn the tables on me? What in the world does he have in store for me next?

* * *

Turns out what he has in store for me is more pastries and more *Star Wars* texts. On Tuesday, I find a basket of palmiers. As I crunch my way through the delicious palm-leaf shaped treats made out of puff pastry, I laugh at one of Pierre's riddles. *What do you get when you cross an elephant with Darth Vader? An ele-Vader.*

I text him back one of my own. *Why did Luke Skywalker cross the road? To get to the Dark Side.*

Good one, he texts back. *Pick you up*

at 10:00 on Saturday?

I send back a GIF of Princess Leia haughtily saying, "no thanks," then shove my phone into my purse for the rest of the day.

* * *

Wednesday's basket is full of éclairs. All kinds of éclairs. Chocolate éclairs so decadent that you moan with pleasure as you eat them. Éclairs filled with a vanilla-flavored crème pâtissière and topped with a salted caramel icing and chopped hazelnuts (my personal favorite; I eat two). Others are crammed full of chestnut puree (definitely not my personal favorite; I only eat one bite), fruit-flavored fillings (the fruit makes them a healthier option, or at least that's what I tell myself), and coffee-flavored whipped cream (the perfect way to get a caffeine buzz).

By the time I work my way through the

basket, I have a tummy ache. I think this is Pierre's plan. Wear me down with stomach pains, then offer to take me to the doctor's office if I say yes to the *Star Wars* convention.

Hah. The joke is on him. My skirt has an elastic band and I'm wearing a loose top. A bloated stomach is not a problem for this girl.

* * *

I come into work late on Thursday. Indigestion can really interfere with one's sleep. While the basket waiting for me on the counter is tempting—it's full of macaroons—I resist.

Pierre sends plenty of texts throughout the day. I'm not sure how he does it. Since he works the night shift, he should be sleeping during the day. I ignore them all. Just like I ignore the macaroons.

The thing is, I don't really like

macaroons, which makes that easy. But when it comes to Pierre, he's a little harder to resist. The Force is strong in this one.

* * *

When I come into work on Friday, I'm greeted by . . . nothing. No pastry basket. No *Star Wars* texts. Nada. Zilch. Zippo. Or *rien*, as the French would say.

Good. Pierre has finally gotten the message. I'm not interested in him or his pastries.

Amélie nudges me. "Mia, I think someone is here to see you."

Han Solo is standing in the doorway. Well, it's not Han Solo himself—he's a fictitious character, after all. No, it's Pierre dressed up as the captain of the *Millennium Falcon*. And, boy, does he look good. Ridiculously good. He sure can pull off the look of an interstellar smuggler—fitted black pants tucked into boots, a white shirt layered under a vest, and a holster slung around his hips.

Pierre winks at me, then spins around. "How do I look?"

"You know exactly how you look," I mutter. "Hot."

"What was that?" he asks.

"You're missing your blaster."

He looks down at his holster. "Oh, I must have left it back at my apartment. But don't worry, I'll have it with me tomorrow."

"Tomorrow?"

"Uh-huh. The Star Wars convention. Since you already have a Princess Leia costume, I thought I'd wear my Han Solo one." He strokes my cheek with his finger and lowers his voice. "You haven't forgotten our date tomorrow, have you, *cherie*?"

Now I know how Princess Leia felt when she was outcharmed by Han Solo. No wonder she let him kiss her on the *Millennium Falcon*.

"Our date," I say slowly.

"Yes, our date," he whispers in my ear.

Then he pulls back, giving me a cocky grin. "Ten o'clock. Don't be late, your highness."

CHAPTER 7
THE BEST LIGHTSABER EVER

My phone buzzes, alerting me to the fact that Pierre will be here any minute now to pick me up. I smooth down my white gown and inspect myself in the full-length mirror. This is one of my favorite Princess Leia costumes. The flowing material, high collar, and bell sleeves flatter my figure, and the flat boots are comfortable.

Everything looks authentic, except for my hair. While I have it styled in the classic cinnamon bun style that Carrie

Fisher wore in the original *Star Wars* movie, my hair is blonde instead of dark brown. I had considered dyeing it last night, but I ran out of time.

After adjusting my metallic belt, I pick up the lightsaber lying on the bed. Should I bring it with me or not? Princes Leia didn't wear a lightsaber with this outfit. It wouldn't be authentic. But, on the other hand, it's a lightsaber. Everything looks better with a lightsaber.

I hear a knock on the door. When I open it, Pierre lets out a low whistle. He motions for me to twirl around, and I oblige. Not because he wants me to, but because I like how my dress swirls around my ankles.

"You look fantastic," he says. "This is my favorite Princess Leia look."

"Hmm. I thought most guys preferred the metal bikini she wore in *Return of the Jedi*."

"Not me. I like it when something is left

to the imagination." He winks at me. "And I have a great imagination."

I step back and examine his outfit. It's the same Han Solo costume that he had on yesterday, but somehow it looks even better today. I twirl my finger in the air. "Fair's fair. Turn around." He spins around, and I realize what's different. He's had a haircut and his shirt doesn't have a collar. The combination of those two things means that the very top of his tattoo is visible when he bends his neck at just the right angle. The black and gray ink is tantalizing. What does the rest of the tattoo look like? As I wonder what lies underneath Pierre's shirt, I realize that I have a pretty great imagination too.

* * *

I don't need a map to know when we've arrived at the convention center. The people standing in line look like they came directly from the set of a *Star Wars* movie. There are the usual costumes—multiple Princess Leias, Luke Skywalkers, and Han Solos—but there are also some fascinating alien creatures. Like the Quarren, who have four tentacles protruding from their jaws, menacing Tusken raiders, and amphibious Gungans.

"Wow, look at that," I say.

"Those guys? Don't you think they're a little tall to pull off Ewok costumes?"

"No, that lightsaber." I pull a napkin out of my backpack and wipe drool off the side of my mouth. Yes, I'm drooling. And, no, I'm not embarrassed because that's how awesome this lightsaber is. Anyone would drool over it.

"You already have one."

My eyes grow wide. "But not like that one. See the intricate carvings on the titanium hilt and the handcrafted blade? That is the ultimate in lightsabers."

"Why don't you buy one?"

"Why don't you buy one?" I say in a mocking tone. "Just like a billionaire. You see something you like and you buy it. You don't think twice about how much it costs. Whatever you want is yours for the taking."

"Who said that I'm a billionaire?"

"It's an educated guess." I tick the evidence off on my fingers. "Boarding school in Britain, custom-made shoes, a polo horse—"

"Who told you I have a polo horse?"

"Amélie."

"I think she might have meant a pool house. We have one at the place in Aruba."

"I stand corrected," I say dryly. "The pool house. Oh, yeah, and there's one other tiny giveaway—you're the heir to the Toussaint fortune."

For once he doesn't look cocky. He takes a deep breath, then exhales slowly. "You're right. I do come from money. And sometimes I forget that not everyone is as fortunate as me. It's something I'm working on. Forgive me?"

I feel his fingers wrap around mine. "You're holding my hand."

He glances down. "Oh, is that what that is? It felt rough and scaly. I thought it was some sort of tentacle."

"My hand isn't rough. I moisturize regularly."

He caresses the back of my hand. "You might need to add an anti-scaling lotion to your beauty routine."

I let out an indignant huff and try to pull my hand away, but he holds on firmly. "I'm just kidding. Your hands are smooth and silky. They feel almost humanlike. I don't think anyone here would suspect that you're really an alien in disguise."

I laugh despite myself. "I'm glad to know that I have everyone fooled. But seriously, you shouldn't be holding my hand."

He furrows his brow. "Why?"

"Because we're in public."

"I'm only holding your hand." He stares intently into my eyes. "It's not like I'm kissing you . . . or worse."

My body tingles as I imagine what he means by "worse." Then I yank my hand away. "I don't believe in public displays of affection."

"Just because you don't believe in something doesn't mean it isn't real. The Force is a prime example. Han Solo doesn't believe in it, but we both know it's real."

I put my hands on my hips. "You know what I mean."

"Fine. I'll just hold your hand and kiss you in private." He leaves the word "worse" unsaid.

* * *

"That panel was amazing," I say as we walk out of the auditorium. "Can you believe Yoda was almost played by a monkey?"

"A monkey could never have pulled that performance off. I'm glad they went with a puppet instead," Pierre says. "Are you hungry?"

"I could eat. Provided it's not croissants. I think I've had my fill of them for a while."

Pierre leads me to the VIP lounge. The attendant takes one look at his pass, then quickly removes the red velvet rope to let us in. As we enter the room, a waiter holds out a tray of crystal glasses.

"*C'est quoi*?" Pierre asks.

"And you call yourself a Star Wars fan," I say. "It's blue and green milk, like they drank in *A New Hope*."

"Yes, miss," the waiter says in halting English. "But it is, how do you say?"

He shoots off rapid-fire French at Pierre, half of which I follow.

"It has a kick to it," Pierre explains. "Like a white Russian."

"Oh, it has liquor in it," I say.

"Which color do you prefer?" Pierre asks.

"Green," I say. "No blue. No, I mean green. No—"

Pierre smiles and takes the tray from the waiter. "Why don't we try them both?"

As I sink into one of the couches scattered around the room, Pierre sets the tray on the coffee table. He sits next to me, then offers me a glass of blue milk. He watches me intently while I sample it. "What do you think?"

"It's good, but I think I need to sample the green to be sure." After a few more sips of each color, I say, "They're both good."

"I prefer the green. I'm surprised you don't have a favorite. You usually have an opinion about everything."

"Well, not everything."

He cocks his head to one side. "Really? What can't you make up your mind about?"

I set my glass down on the table. No more milk for me. The alcohol is going to my head and I'm afraid if I have any more, I'll babble out something I'll regret, like "You. I can't make up my mind about you. You've got a geeky quality that I love, but you're also rich. And rich guys can't be trusted."

"You seem to have a problem with my background," he says.

"What are you talking about?"

"You just said that rich guys can't be trusted."

My face grows warm. "I said that out loud?"

"Yes. Your enunciation was crystal clear. You don't trust me because of the family I was born into. But it's not like I chose my parents. Did you choose yours?"

"Well, of course not."

"Would you change your background if you could?"

"No, not at all," I say firmly. "Sure, my parents can be annoying, and they don't understand why I want to work in the art world, but they gave me the values and work ethic that I have today."

"Amélie talks about your work ethic all the time."

"All the time? How often do you see her?"

"I go to their place once a week for dinner. Jean-Paul and Amélie are like second parents to me." He strokes his chin. "You should come one night."

"You can't invite me to dinner at someone else's place."

"That's true. I should invite you to dinner at my place."

"Oh, you want me to come to your mansion?"

"I don't live in a mansion. I live in an apartment, just like normal people."

I raise my eyebrows. "Normal people? Let me ask you something. Do you have a doorman at your apartment building?"

He nods, looking abashed. "Okay, then, not exactly like normal people."

The silence gets awkward and I'm glad when a waiter comes by bearing a tray of canapés.

"Oh, mousse de saumon," Pierre says. "They're my favorite. You have to try it."

He hands me a small slice of rye bread spread with a spread of smoked salmon, sour cream, and lemon juice. I devour it in two bites. He smiles and hands me another. This one I scarf down in just one bite.

Pierre's eyes light up. "Ah, I see escargot over there."

As he waves the waiter over, I gulp. It's going to take a lot of blue and green milk before I work up the courage to eat snails.

Fortunately, by the time the waiter comes over, he's out of escargot. I breathe a sigh of relief. Before Pierre can search out another waiter with a tray loaded up with slimy garden pests, I distract him by pointing out an adorable toddler dressed up as Yoda. His mother is crouched on the floor, taking pictures as he walks toward her. When he tumbles to the ground and starts bawling, she rushes over and soothes him.

"Oh, poor thing," I say.

Pierre presses his fingers against the bridge of his nose and breathes rapidly, almost as though he's hyperventilating.

"Don't worry. He'll be fine. Toddlers fall all the time. It's part of learning to walk." When the boy's mother tickles his belly, and he giggles, I say, "See, all better."

"It's not better," Pierre says, his voice cracking. "It will never be better."

I place my hand on Pierre's arm and give him a gentle squeeze. "Hey, what's going on?"

He takes a few deep breaths, then says softly, "I'm sorry. They reminded me of something, that's all."

"Who? The mom and her son? What do they remind you of?"

"They remind me of my mother." Pierre drains the contents of his glass. "Of my birth mother. Today is the anniversary of the day when she abandoned me and my father. I was that boy's age. Seeing how sweet his *maman* is with him . . ."

He picks up another glass of milk, considers it, then sets it back on the tray. He slumps back into the couch and stares vacantly into space.

I'm at a loss. What do you say when someone tells you that their mother left him? Turns out, I don't need to say anything. Pierre twists his body around to face me, then tells me everything. He barely pauses to catch a breath. I learn how devastated his father was. He didn't know how to deal with raising a small child. So there were nannies and boarding school. His father kept his distance, engrossing himself in his work, acquiring hotels across the globe.

"Things got better when my father met my mother," Pierre says.

I furrow my brow. "Met your mother? You mean she came back?"

"No, my birth mother died shortly after she left us, in a tragic accident. The woman I'm talking about is technically my stepmother, but I think of her as my mother. They got married when I was eight years old. My father refers to her as his lioness. She's fierce. She'll do anything to protect us."

"I'd love to meet her."

"Would you?" Pierre chuckles softly. "Then come with me to the charity ball on Saturday night."

I shake my head. "A charity ball? That really doesn't sound like my cup of tea."

"But it's for a good cause. We're raising money for orphanages in Africa."

"I'd rather make a donation than get dressed up and make small talk with people I don't know."

"Do it for me."

His hazel eyes are twinkling again, and I'm almost tempted to say yes. But I have too many unpleasant memories of going to charity balls at the country club with my ex. His family and friends looked at me with disdain, making it clear that they thought I came from the wrong side of the tracks.

Pierre grabs my hands and caresses them. "Please, do it for me. I have to give a speech and I'm nervous about it. If you're by my side, I'll—"

"You? Nervous? You practically reek of self-confidence."

"I guess I'm a good actor. Maybe they should cast me in the next *Star Wars* film."

I grin. "I'd love to see you wear a Wookie costume."

"I bet you would. All that fur. A total turn-on." He gives me a smile that makes my toes curl, then turns more serious. "I took a year off after college and spent it working in Africa at an orphanage. The experience was . . ." He struggles to find the words to express the impact it had on him. Finally, he says, "Actually, it doesn't matter what I got out of the experience. What matters is helping children who have lost their parents. I set up this charity to raise money for orphanages across Africa. This is our inaugural fundraiser. Hence, the speech. Hence, my nerves. Hence, I want you by my side."

"That's a lot of 'hences,'" I joke, trying to lighten the mood.

"So, *hence,* you're coming?"

"I'll be there."

He leans in, and I panic that he's going to kiss me in public. When his phone buzzes, I scoot off the couch and perch on a chair, the coffee table creating a barrier between the two of us. He laughs at my reaction.

I watch as he has a one-sided conversation with the person on the other end of the line. His responses are mostly variations of *"oui"* and *"non."* After hanging up, he taps on his phone pensively for a moment, then turns to me. "I'm so sorry, I have to go. Some urgent family business has come up. Let me get you a taxi to take you back to the hotel."

I wave him away. "No need. I can take the Métro."

He glances at his watch. "Are you sure?"

"I'll be fine. Go."

He leans down and gives me a kiss on the cheek, then rushes off. I slouch back in the chair and sip on my blue milk. I've certainly learned a lot about Pierre this afternoon. His mother abandoning him, the charity work he does in Africa, and the fact that he thinks green milk tastes better than blue. But there are a few things I still need to find out about—the injury that meant he couldn't play rugby anymore, why he worked as a waiter on the cruise ship rather than at one of his family's hotels, and, perhaps most importantly, what the tattoo on his back looks like.

CHAPTER 8
TOILET PAPER MISHAPS

On the way to the charity ball, Pierre talks to his father on the phone. I know that he's disappointed his dad can't make it tonight, but he understands that the grand opening of a new Toussaint hotel in Thailand takes precedence.

While they chat, I amuse myself pushing buttons on the console next to me. The only other time I've been in a limousine was at my senior prom. Actually, it wasn't so much a limo as it was a converted hearse. While it did have a mini-bar, it was seriously grim compared to this sleek town car.

As he says goodbye to his dad, Pierre squeezes my hand. "I'm glad you came tonight. Isabelle thought you might try to get out of it."

"Isabelle? When did you speak to her?"

"I texted her yesterday."

I furrow my brow. "Why exactly?"

"I needed some info."

"Info about what?"

He leans over and playfully tugs my earlobe. "About you."

"Whoa. Wait, a minute. You're texting *my* friend to get information about me?" I pull out my phone and dial her number.

"That won't do you any good," Pierre says, glancing at his watch. "She just started her shift."

"How come you know her work schedule?"

"I know lots of things. For example, I know about the volunteer work you did back home, and I know all about this guy Isabelle just met. To be honest, I'm not so sure about him."

I hold up my hands, at a loss for where to start. What else has Isabelle told him, and how come I don't know about this guy she met?

"I think it's pretty amazing what you did," Pierre says. "Not everyone would volunteer to work with guys like that. That's pretty brave."

"Everyone needs a second chance," I say quietly. "Isabelle shouldn't have told you about that. It's not something I like to tell people about."

"Don't worry, it will be our little secret."

"Well, I hope you're better at keeping secrets than Isabelle is."

As we pull up to the hotel where the charity ball is being held—also a Toussaint property—I take a deep breath. I watch as a glamorous couple gets out of the car in front of us. The woman's evening dress is haute couture, the diamonds dangling from her ears are the size of golf balls, and her hair and makeup are runway ready.

My dress is off-the-rack. Seriously off-the-rack. I literally found it on the floor in a second-hand shop. After steaming the wrinkles out and strategically placing a rhinestone broach over a stain, it was as good as new. Just not as good as haute couture.

My jewelry consists of a necklace my parents gave me for my eighteenth birthday. It might not be encrusted with diamonds, but its value is priceless to me. My hair and makeup, on the other hand, might just pass muster. Amélie helped me get ready, putting my hair into an elegant updo and giving my face an evening look that's chic and timeless.

After Monsieur and Madame Glamour pose for the photographers, our car advances to the entryway. I start to open the passenger door, but Pierre tells me to wait while the chauffeur walks around to my door. I feel like I'm in a fairy tale when he helps me out of the car.

Pierre takes over after that, tucking my hand through his arm and escorting me across the red carpet to the hotel entrance. As we pause for photographs, I whisper, "The volunteer work I do is nothing compared to this."

He puts his arm around me and draws me toward him. In hushed tones, he says, "In all honesty, this is just an excuse for people to get dressed up, show off, and feel good about themselves because they donated money to a good cause. Most of them are oblivious to the harsh realities that the orphans they're supporting have to deal with."

"But you're raising money."

"Yes, but it costs a lot to put on an event like this. Besides, money isn't everything."

As we make our way inside, I think

about what he's said. If push came to shove, would Pierre really think that money isn't everything? Looking around at the wealth and opulence surrounding me, I'm not so sure.

* * *

"You sure you'll be okay on your own?" Pierre asks.

We're standing at the front of the ballroom, and the hotel staff wants to test Pierre's microphone. "I'll be fine," I say. "It's not like I'm the shy, retiring type."

He grins. "No, you certainly aren't."

Actually, I am feeling a little nervous about mingling with this crowd, but there's no way I'm going to let Pierre know that. He has a speech to give, and the last thing he needs to worry about is me. "Go shake your money-maker," I say.

"I'll find you as soon as it's over," he

says over his shoulder as he's whisked away.

I try talking to a few people, but not even the waiters passing out champagne will give me the time of day. Maybe I have lipstick smudged on my teeth? Maybe there's a stain on my dress that I didn't notice? Maybe they're all just a bunch of snobs.

Feeling my eyes well up, I do what women have done since the invention of modern plumbing. Rush to the ladies' room to hide.

It takes me a while to find it, not helped by the fact that everyone pretends that they can't understand me when I ask them to point in the right direction. I may not be fluent in French, but I know enough to be able to ask where *la toilette* is. I even mimed what I was looking for, pointing at the general direction of my bladder, without any success.

Eventually, I stumble across the

ladies' room. Although it does take me a while to figure out that's what it is. That's because the place is bigger than my parents' entire house. I have to wander through several rooms before I find the one containing toilet stalls. I don't need to go to the bathroom, but I do need the privacy it offers to regroup and get a hold of myself.

I perch on the edge of the toilet and stare at the door. Unlike many of the restrooms I'm used to, this one doesn't have things scrawled on it, like "Mandy loves Steve," "I like writing on walls," and "Believe in yourself."

Thank goodness for cell phones. You can text your friends for moral support even while hiding out in the ladies' room in an opulent hotel in Paris. I open my evening bag and pull mine out, then utter a curse. A fancy place like this doesn't have cell phone coverage? Unbelievable.

I wipe away a tear forming at the

corner of my eye. *Get a hold of yourself, Mia. You need to go out there and support Pierre. You can do it.*

Another tear threatens to fall down my cheek and ruin my makeup. As I go to pull a piece of toilet paper off to dab at it, I hear a low growl. Lyonette, the hotel director's poodle, tunnels her way under the door, then grabs the end of the toilet paper from my hand and yanks hard.

Of course, they have high-quality toilet paper at this hotel. If you yanked at the toilet paper at my apartment back home, the roll purchased on sale at the local dollar store, it'd tear off easily. No, this stuff is industrial strength, while having a soft, luxurious feel—yeah, I don't know how they do that either.

"Hey, hang on a minute," I say to Lyonette. "Toilet paper is for humans, not dogs."

The dog gives me some serious side eye. Then she barks sharply at me. Her meaning is clear. "This toilet paper isn't meant for humans like you. Your derriere isn't worthy."

She tunnels back under the door, the toilet paper unwinding behind her. I push the door open to chase after her and run straight into the woman I least want to see—Lyonette's owner. Go figure. She's surrounded by a posse of glamorous women, all staring at me like I'm an alien from one of the *Star Wars* movie.

In between giving me disdainful looks, they take turns commenting on my appearance. They're speaking in French, probably assuming that the barbarian in front of them can't understand. But I do. Let's just say their comments aren't flattering.

I bite my tongue. You have no idea how hard this is, but the last thing I need is to lose my temper in front of the director, and then lose my job. Funny how not too long ago I would have walked away from the job and Pierre, but now . . . something's changed.

The director gives me an appraising look, but says nothing. After a beat, she summons Lyonette, then turns on her heel and walks out of the room, her posse following in her wake.

Two good things have come out of this incident. First, it's reminded me not to give a hoot what other people think of me. And, second, that stupid dog pranced out of the ladies' room with toilet paper stuck to her paw. Imagine how embarrassed she's going to be when she realizes it.

* * *

As he finishes his speech, Pierre locks eyes with me. I'm standing at the back of the ballroom, but I can see him winking from here. Making a fist pump in the air, I yell, "Whoot-whoot." He did such an amazing job. Eloquent, self-effacing, and inspiring, all wrapped up in one delectable package.

As I let out another "whoot-whoot," Lyonette rushes over and alternates between growling and barking at me. If she didn't look like she was about to fly at me in a rabid rage, I'd almost think the toilet paper stuck to her paw was comical.

A woman sitting at the table in front of me turns and gives me an icy stare. She calls Lyonette over and scratches her on the head, telling her what a good doggy she is. Why this pretentious poodle deserves praise is beyond me.

I wait while Pierre makes his way toward me. It takes him a while as people stop to congratulate him. I hope they're also handing him fistfuls of euros for the orphanages. When he eventually reaches me, he brushes his fingers up my arms, across my shoulders, then cups my face in his hands.

Before he can kiss me, I turn my head. "Whoa, not here, mister. Half of

France's upper crust, along with one very obnoxious poodle, are watching."

"But the French are very passionate people. They see nothing wrong with kissing a beautiful woman in public."

"This isn't about them. This is about me." I twist my body, slipping out of his grasp. Pointing at the nearest exit, I lead him out of the ballroom and into the adjacent courtyard. Looking around to make sure we're not observed, I pull him behind a large trellis of roses that hides us from view.

I smile. "Well, what are you waiting for?"

"Is this the American version of hide and seek?" He jokes as he peeks around the trellis. "Can we play tag next?"

"Yeah, tag, you're it." I punch him playfully. I feel his bicep tense as my knuckles graze him. I slowly unclench my fist, raking my fingers against his muscular arm. He shivers and his breath quickens. With my other hand, I do the same thing on his other arm. Then I trace a path with my fingernails from each of his arms to the center of his chest. When I reach the middle, I grab his lapels, pulling him toward me.

"I like how you Americans play tag."

Then he kisses me. It isn't a gentle kiss. It isn't a tentative kiss. It's the kind of kiss a man gives someone when he knows exactly what he wants. And he wants me.

He presses me against the wall, his kiss leaving me breathless.

The sensation is overwhelming.

Suddenly, he pulls back. His hazel eyes are unreadable. He holds his hands up as if he's surrendering.

I inhale sharply. Is he going to say this is a mistake? Is he going to make a hasty departure? My stomach is twisted in knots. He stares at me for a beat, then a cocky grin slowly spreads across his face.

He taps me on the arm. "Tag, you're it."

So I kiss him. It isn't a gentle kiss. It isn't a tentative kiss. It's the kind of kiss a woman gives someone when she knows exactly what she wants. And I want him.

I pull him toward me, my kiss leaving him breathless.

The sensation overwhelms me. I have no doubt that the sensation overwhelms him too.

Then a woman's sharp voice says, "Lyonette, *ici*," and I'm overwhelmed by a completely different sensation—fear. Fear of being discovered.

I send a silent prayer up to the gods of hide and seek—*Please don't let that horrible dog find us*.

The gods are apparently playing their own game of hide and seek because they're nowhere to be found. Lyonette barrels toward us, knocking down the trellis in the process.

"Pierre," the woman snaps.

Oh, no. I know that voice. It's the hotel director. Encountering her in the ladies' room was bad enough. Now she and her interfering poodle have to turn up and ruin everything.

I try to burrow into Pierre's chest. I'm short. Maybe she won't see me.

No such luck. Pierre turns, leaving me exposed. I give a half-hearted wave. She ignores me. Her dog, on the other hand, bares her teeth and growls.

Pierre smiles at the director, bending down to kiss her on each cheek. Then he turns and formally introduces me to her. "*Maman, je te présente Mia. Elle travaille à la galerie d'art.*"

You don't have to be fluent in French to understand the critical word in that sentence—*maman*. The director of the hotel is Pierre's mother. She may not have given birth to him, but she's the woman he considers to be his mom. Fluency in French isn't required to translate her response either. Her body language makes it crystal clear—she's going to do everything in her power to keep the two of us apart.

CHAPTER 9
SWEATING IN A SNOWSUIT

Pierre's mother crooks her perfectly manicured finger at him, then turns and walks briskly back into the ballroom. Lyonette trots along next to her, the toilet paper stuck to her paw flicking back and forth.

Pierre loosens his bowtie, then runs his fingers through his sandy-brown hair. "I better go talk to her. Wait for me here?"

He doesn't wait for my response. To be honest, I don't know how I would have replied.

I could have said something like, "Sure, no problem. I'll stay here and twiddle my thumbs while you explain to your mother why you're making out with an American girl who is clearly unsuited to your social standing."

Or maybe something along the lines of, "You don't seriously expect me to wait around while you run off with your tail between your legs like some sort of mama's boy? No way, buddy, I'm out of here."

I'm torn. Should I stay or should I go? With an old song from the punk rock band, The Clash, playing through my head, I weigh up the pros and cons.

If I go, then Pierre will know that I'm no pushover. He'll get the message that I'm a strong woman who does just fine on her own, thank you very much.

I smooth down my dress, straighten my shoulders, and inhale deeply. Yes, that's exactly what I'm going to do. I'm going to march on out of here, head held high.

But as I turn to leave, my stomach starts growling. "Hey, wait a minute, Mia," it says. "If you leave, you're going to miss a seriously good meal. Lobster bisque to start, followed by steak au poivre, and finished off with apple tarte tatin. You don't want to skip that, do you? You can swallow your pride and stay, can't you? For little old me, please?"

I pat my tummy. "With all the pastries I've been eating, you're not all that little anymore. Besides, we don't want Pierre to assume he has me wrapped around his little finger, do we? He didn't even wait for my answer. He just assumed that I'd stay here, fixed to this spot, waiting for him to return."

"Well, I guess you do have a point," my stomach says, in between loud gurgles. "But, if we go, can we stop at that kebab place on the way back to the hotel?"

My heart decides to intervene. "Enough with this food talk. We're talking about how Mia feels, not how hungry you are." Beating rapidly, it adds, "This is exactly like what happened at that Halloween dance Mia and her ex went to."

I put my head in my hands, flashbacks to that night flooding my brain.

Naturally, the Halloween dance had been held at the country club. No surprise there. Folks like my ex don't exactly rent out the high school gym and rely on the local sub shop for catering when they have a party. Nope, they need valets to park their cars, attendants in the restrooms to hand them towels, and waiters to ensure the champagne keeps flowing.

I remember being so excited about my costume. I spent hours making a replica of the white snowsuit Princess Leia wore on the planet Hoth, keeping it a secret from my ex. When he picked me up, I twirled around, a huge grin on my face. But his only reaction was to raise his eyebrows and say, "Don't you think you're going to be hot?"

When we got to the country club, he was distant. Normally, I had to fend off his public displays of affection, but this time, he didn't even try to hold my hand. After getting me a drink, he told me to wait for me at the bar while he spoke with someone about an important business deal.

By "someone," he meant all the women in attendance. I watched as he flirted with the girls my age—all of whom were dressed up in sexy, skin-revealing costumes—fawned over the married ladies, and schmoozed the elderly widows.

I waited, and waited, and waited. Eventually, I had to remove my parka, totally ruining my Princess Leia look. He had been right. I was boiling. Boiling from how hot it was in the bar and boiling from rage as he continued to ignore me.

Eventually, his mother took pity on me. At least that's what, in my naivety, I thought it was at the time. But it really was condescension. While I wiped sweat off my brow, she suggested I go home and change into something more comfortable. She even offered to have her chauffeur take me back to my apartment, and then, once I was ready, she suggested that I text her son to come pick me up.

You can probably figure out what happened. I went home. I changed my clothes. I texted my ex to come get me. I waited for him to respond. I waited for him some more. I texted him again and waited even more. Eventually, I fell asleep on the couch, clutching my lightsaber to my chest like a security blanket.

A low growl jolts me back to the

present. This time it isn't my stomach; it's Lyonette. The poodle is sniffing at the hem of my dress. Then she crouches on the ground near me, fixing her beady eyes on me, as if to say, "Have I got a little surprise for you."

I narrow my eyes. "Don't you dare pee on my dress."

Stepping back just in time, I scowl as she finishes her bio-break. When she's done, she scratches the flagstone patio, then barks sharply at me. Her meaning is clear. "Snap to it and clean this mess up, loser."

I give her the finger. Yes, that's what it's come to; I'm flipping dogs off. Realizing that the evening isn't going to get any better, I hightail it out of there, leaving Lyonette to find some other human to do her bidding.

* * *

Pierre texted me that night, asking

where I had disappeared to. Rather than get into it, I told him that I had eaten one too many hors d'oeuvres and went home with an upset stomach. They say that if you're going to lie to someone, to base it on a partial truth. I *had* eaten too many hors d'oeuvres. Who can say no to crème fraîche tartlets? Or caramelized figs topped with smoky bacon? Not this girl. Plus, there was that kebab that I ate on the way back to the hotel. That didn't help matters.

The next day, it was easy to make excuses for not catching up. Pierre was busy with a board meeting for his charity during the day, then he worked the night shift. I was occupied at the art gallery with a constant stream of customers during the day, followed by spending the evening putting together promotional materials for the upcoming photography exhibition.

But now it's Monday, and I can't avoid him any longer. Probably because he's standing right in front of me holding a chocolate croissant.

"Is your stomach feeling better?" he asks, waving it under my nose.

The smell of chocolate is intoxicating. So is the smell of Pierre's cologne. I want them both. But I know that only one of these two temptations is good for me.

So I grab the high-calorie pastry from his hand.

He laughs while I cram it in my mouth. Ladylike I am not, especially when it comes to chocolate croissants.

"I guess you are feeling better. Dinner tonight?" he asks. "I know a place that serves the best cassoulet outside of Carcossonne."

I tap the glossy catalog on the counter. "Sorry, I have to proofread this so that we can get changes made in time for the opening night of the photography exhibition."

Yes, that was only partially true. I do

have to review the catalog, but there's time before I have to get the final changes to the printer.

After Pierre leaves, Amélie gives me a stern look. "If you don't want to go out with him, you should just say so."

"It's not that I don't want to go out with him, it's that I don't want to . . ."

"Don't want to what, *chérie?*"

I opt for the full truth this time. "I don't want to fall for him."

She gives me a wry smile. "I think it's too late for that."

I chew on my lip. She's right. Not only am I telling fibs to Pierre, I'm lying to myself.

"Okay, I admit it," I say. "I like him. But I'm definitely not head over heels—"

"Head over heels? What does this mean?"

I scratch my head, trying to figure out how to explain the expression to her. Learning idioms in foreign languages is so hard, at least for me. Like, *"avoir un coup de foudre,"* which literally means to be struck by lightning. But its idiomatic meaning is "to fall in love at first sight." Not that I know anything about that. No, sirree. I'm not in love with Pierre. I'm just attracted to him.

"Head over heels?" Amélie prompts.

"It's when you're so madly in love with someone that it feels like you're tumbling head over heels."

Amélie still looks perplexed. "Tumbling?"

Sometimes, it's easier to demonstrate something than explain it. I look around to make sure that we're the only ones in the gallery. Then I do a somersault.

Okay, talk about a really bad decision. As my back strikes the floor, I realize that marble is really hard. There was a reason why we used padded mats back when I did gymnastics. I think I'm going to need chiropractic treatment after this. Being impetuous isn't all it's cracked up to be. If Isabelle had been in my situation, she would have thought through this carefully, decided demonstrating a somersault was extremely misguided, and figured out how to explain "head over heels" with actual words, rather than her body.

As I complete the somersault, I realize that this is actually worse than a bad decision. Pierre's mother is standing there, her jaw slack.

But, wait, it gets even worse. Lyonette is right by her side. Apparently, she interprets my gymnastic move as an invitation to play with her chew toy. And guess who her chew toy is.

* * *

I grab a wet washcloth from the bathroom in the back and sponge dog drool off my face and arms. It's going to be harder to fix the rips in my top.

Amélie knocks on the door. "It's safe to come out. They're gone."

I peek out, making sure there aren't any vicious dogs lying in wait. Who knows? Lyonette could have been holding a gun to Amélie's head, forcing her to tell me that the coast is clear. Realizing that the lack of opposable thumbs might make hostage-taking a challenge, even for the most determined poodle, I finally step out of the bathroom.

When Amélie sees me, she removes her cardigan and hands it to me. "This will hide the tears in your blouse. *La directrice d'hôtel* will have a replacement sent to your room later today."

"Pierre's mother is going to replace my top? I find that hard to believe."

"Why?" Amélie seems genuinely puzzled.

"Uh, well, she could have stopped her dog from attacking me in the first place."

"Attacking you? *Non*, the dog was playing. That means that she likes you.

She does that all the time with Pierre. It is, what do you call it . . . tough-homing?"

"You mean rough-housing?"

She nods, repeating the expression slowly. "Knowing her, *la directrice* will most likely send you several new blouses. And they will all be designer labels."

"Of course, they will be," I say dryly. "That's probably why she sicced her dog on me. She thinks my off-the-rack clothes aren't good enough to work here at the hotel."

Amélie cocks her head to one side. "*Au contraire.* She appreciates people who have a unique sense of style like you do. It would not matter to her where you got your clothes."

"With people like her, that's all that matters."

"I think, perhaps, that is because you do not know her." Amélie leans in and lowers her voice. "She shows a tough exterior to the world, but there is good reason for that. She is a lioness. She protects those closest to her. Sometimes, that comes off as cold and hard, but, I promise you, that is not what she is like inside."

I don't want to get into an argument with Amélie. Ever since I came to Paris, she's taken me under her wing and given me the most amazing opportunities. "I'll have to take your word for it," I say evenly.

Her phone rings. "Ah, it is Madame Vernier. I have to take this."

While Amélie chats with Madame Vernier about catering for the opening night reception, I flip through the proof copy of the exhibition catalog. The photographs that will be displayed are amazing. It's art at multiple levels—the art created by tattooists using ink on skin and the interpretation of that art by the photographers through their camera lenses.

Amélie hangs up the phone and turns to me, a playful smile on her lips. "It is a good thing you told Pierre you are busy tonight."

I furrow my brow. A few minutes ago, Amélie was chastising me for lying to Pierre.

"I need you to go to the Voodoo Hoodoo Tattoo Parlor tonight. One of our featured tattoo artists is going to be there, and a photographer is going to be there to take pictures of him in action. I need you to be there to coordinate everything." She gives me a teasing look. "Unless you'd rather stay here and proofread the catalog?"

"No way. Visiting the Voodoo Hoodoo has been on my list of things to do in Paris. Count me in. Who's the tattoo artist?"

"Dominic de Santis."

I squeal like a guinea pig. And I'm not ashamed of it either. Dominic de Santis is my tattoo artist crush. My idol. If I could be a tenth as good as him, I'd be ecstatic.

As I twirl around in circles, squealing and clapping my hands together, Amélie laughs. Then she says more seriously, "You don't mind if Monsieur de Santis does a small tattoo on you for the photographs, do you? They want to document his process."

I gulp, realizing that I've never told Amélie that I don't have any tattoos of my own, let alone why. What would she think if I told her I'm afraid of needles? Heck, what would Dominic de Santis think? I don't know of any other tattoo artists who don't have tattoos. Is it time for me to bite the bullet and get one of my own?

* * *

When I arrive at Voodoo Hoodoo, I pause on the sidewalk and take it all in. Its quirkiness fits in with the other buildings on this uber-cool street. The building is painted black, the door is a glossy cherry apple red, and the shutters are made out of corrugated metal. But what really catches my eye are the hundreds of voodoo dolls that have been attached to the exterior.

I step closer to examine the dolls, shuddering when I see the pins stuck through some of them. It's not much different from getting inked—tiny needles being inserted into your skin. Can I really go through with getting a tattoo? Even if it's the world-renowned Dominic de Santis who would be doing it? How many people can say that they have a Dominic de Santis tat on their body? It doesn't get any more prestigious than that.

Why are you being so indecisive? Get a grip. This is a huge career opportunity for you. I take a deep breath and push open the door.

"Are you Mia?" a young woman with

pink dreadlocks asks. "Madame Vernier said you would be helping out tonight."

When she holds out her hand to shake mine, I admire the watercolor-style tattoo that wraps around her forearm. Pastel flowers are interspersed with tropical birds. "The subtle shifts in color are amazing," I say.

"Thanks," she says. "One of the tattoo artists here did it for me."

"Do you work here?"

She nods. "I'm an apprentice."

"I remember my apprenticeship," I say. "Those two years just flew by."

"I'm going to start working on skin next week."

"That's so exciting." She gives me a faint smile while she fidgets with her large silver earrings. "Don't worry, you'll be fine. They wouldn't let you near skin if they didn't think you could do it."

"I hope you're right." After pulling her dreadlocks back into a colorful hair tie, she says, "Come on, let me introduce you to Dominic."

She leads me over to a small seating area at the back of the tattoo parlor. Dominic is sitting on a red velvet couch, sipping on a glass of sparkling water. After introductions, he motions for me to sit next to him.

"I was very happy when Madame Vernier arranged for you to be here," he says.

His Italian accent reminds me of Lorenzo, the guy who Isabelle and I rented an apartment from in Ravenna. But that's where the similarity ends. While Lorenzo looks like a male model, Dominic is the spitting image of my Uncle Joe. Short, balding, and wearing a polyester leisure suit straight from the 1970s. Uncle Joe wears leisure suits to all of our family gatherings. It's a look he adopted in the previous century and hasn't deviated from since. Dominic's leisure suit, on the other hand, screams quirky vintage, clearly meant to be an ironic fashion statement.

After offering me a glass of water, he gets down to business. "The photographer will be here soon. I'd like you to coordinate with him. It's essential that he understand the process of *tatouage* so that he can truly capture the essence of what we do. Because you are a tattoo artist, you will be able to explain things to him."

I bite my lip. He just called me a tattoo artist. Without a doubt tattoos are an art form, but am I an artist? Until today, I had always referred to myself as a tattoo artist. But now I'm sitting in the presence of Dominic de Santis, a man whose designs are legendary and whose skill at applying tattoos is unparalleled.

As if he can read my mind, he tells me that he's seen my portfolio. "I admire how you take paintings by the Old Masters and reinterpret them as tattoos. I was particularly intrigued by your take on Johannes Vermeer's *The Girl with the Pearl Earring*. Replacing the pearl with a skull and weaving a subtle pattern of insects into the dress the girl is wearing was genius."

"Really?" I stammer.

"You apprenticed under Henry Tusk, didn't you?" I nod. "He taught you well."

I take a sip of my water, stalling for time. I have no idea how to respond without babbling like an idiot. Dominic de Santis knows my work *and* he likes it. The bubbles tickle my nose. As I stifle a sneeze, I realize that there's only one thing I can say.

"Can I have your babies?"

I'm kidding. Of course, I don't say that. Although, the idea of plump little babies wearing polyester leisure suits makes me giggle. If I ever decide to make a career change, that's going to be it— designing retro babywear.

What I do say is, "Tattoo me."

And I mean it. I'm ready to get my first

tattoo. Needles or no needles. I am going to overcome my fear.

Dominic looks taken aback. I guess it did come out like some sort of weird command.

"Madame Vernier said that you were going to do a small tattoo on me for the photographs," I say, the stammer back in my voice.

"Ah, yes, that was the original plan. But I have another model lined up. You are more valuable to me coordinating with the photographer since you know about *tatouage*." Dominic sets his glass down on the coffee table. "My assistant should be finished prepping the workstation and getting the model ready. Come, I will introduce you."

I follow Dominic into an adjacent room. A man is lying on a table face down. My eyes travel from his form-fitting jeans, up to his muscular back, and then to the sandy-brown hair on his head. While the assistant wipes the model's right shoulder blade with alcohol, I notice a tattoo on the base of the man's neck.

As I lean closer to examine it, Dominic says, "The shading of the elephant's ear is exquisite, don't you think?"

"The use of gray tones is stunning," I say. "Is it one of yours?"

"I wish I could take credit," he says. "But, alas, I cannot."

"What kind of tattoo are you doing today?" I ask.

While Dominic washes his hands, the assistant shows me the design.

My jaw drops. "Is that what I think it is? A yellow-bellied marmot?"

The man lying on the table turns his head and looks at me. His hazel eyes sparkle in the overhead lights.

"Pierre . . . you're the model?"

"I guess you don't have to work on the catalog after all tonight, Mia," he says. Then he winks at me.

CHAPTER 10
PLANES, TRAINS, AND BABBLING IDIOTS

"So let me get this straight. You got Pierre to strip down for you?" Ginny asks.

Isabelle chimes in. "Exactly how naked was he?"

I'm stretched out on my bed, video chatting with my two friends. After the session at the tattoo parlor finished, I texted the two of them a picture of Pierre's back so that they could see the elephant tattoo on the base of his neck, as well as the new marmot tattoo inked by Dominic de Santis. Within seconds, they both texted back, wanting to get the full scoop.

"He wasn't naked," I say. "He only had his shirt off."

"So, half-naked," Isabelle says.

I roll my eyes. "Stop using the word 'naked.' You're making it sound dirty. It was purely professional. He was getting a tattoo and I was—"

"Drooling over his half-naked body," Isabelle says.

"I wasn't drooling," I say. "I was . . ."

"Salivating?" Isabelle suggests.

"Isn't that just another word for drooling?" I ask.

Isabelle shakes her head. "No, drooling is when saliva drips out of your mouth."

Ginny shudders. "Please don't talk about drooling. I just had a cat drool all over me. It's disgusting."

"Where are you, anyway?" I ask her.

"That doesn't look like Boston in the background."

"I'm in Florida, visiting my mom," Ginny says.

"Is Preston with you?" I ask.

"Hang on a minute. We can talk about Ginny and Preston later. But first, I want to hear more about Pierre getting naked for Mia," Isabelle teases. "He looks pretty hot in that picture."

I prop up the pillow underneath my head. "Doesn't Dominic do fabulous work? I'm in awe of how he's incorporating Pierre's scar into the tattoo. See how he's turning it into the rock that the marmot is perched on? I can't wait to see how the tattoo looks once it's completed."

"How did Pierre get that scar, anyway?" Isabelle asks.

"I'm not sure," I say. "It wasn't exactly the time or place to ask him."

"But you are going to ask him, right?" Isabelle asks before taking a sip from her wineglass.

"What are you drinking?" I ask.

"Riesling." She holds up the glass so that we can get a better view. "In the Rhine and Moselle regions, this is what you traditionally serve Riesling in. It's called a Roemer glass. See the green stem and how it looks coiled?"

Ginny interrupts. "Isabelle, as much as I'd love to talk about the historical origins of the glass you're drinking out of, you do realize that Mia's trying to change the subject by getting you to talk about wine instead of Pierre, right?"

Isabelle laughs. "Very sneaky, Mia. Let's get back to your sexy Frenchman. When are you going to see him next?"

"Well, as I was leaving Voodoo Hoodoo, I got a call from Amélie. She's sending me to one of the Toussaint hotels in Carcassonne tomorrow so that I can set up an art display at their gift store."

"Where's Carcassonne?" Isabelle

asks.

"It's in southwestern France, about fifty miles east of Toulouse."

Ginny gets a dreamy look in her eye. "I would love to go to Carcassonne. Did you know that the area has been occupied since Neolithic times? It was also strategically important to the Romans."

"You're such a history nerd," I joke.

"And you're a *Star Wars* nerd," she retorts.

Isabelle pipes up. "Just for the record, I don't have any nerdish qualities whatsoever."

"Yeah, that's a serious character flaw," I say.

She rolls her eyes. "I just googled Carcassonne. The place looks like it came straight out of a fairy tale. There's a castle with turrets and a drawbridge."

"That's the walled medieval city," Ginny says. "It's a UNESCO World Heritage Site."

"It's so romantic," Isabelle says. "You think you'd be happy being sent on a business trip there, Mia. All expenses paid, right?"

"Uh-huh," I say flatly.

After a beat, Isabelle says. "Oh, my gosh, I know what's going on. Pierre is going to be there too, isn't he?"

I nod. "His father asked him to attend a meeting on his behalf at the hotel."

"I thought he was a bellboy," Ginny says.

"He is. But while his father is away in Thailand, Pierre has to fill in for him at certain management events. Just my luck one of them happens to be in Carcassonne at the same exact time I'll be there."

"Good, that will give you an opportunity to ask him how he got that scar," Ginny says. "And if you're lucky, maybe he'll take off his shirt again so that you can examine it more closely."

"Do you think he has scars anyplace

else?" Isabelle asks.

"Looks like I'm losing cell phone reception," I say, making a crackling sound with a crumpled up piece of paper. Then I quickly hang up before they start talking about Pierre removing any other of his clothing items.

* * *

There are times when I'm glad I'm afraid of flying, and this is one of them. Pierre needed to be in Carcassonne early, so he flew there on the company's private plane. A pretty flight attendant probably served him mimosas while he nibbled on freshly baked croissants. When he landed, a chauffeur was likely there waiting for him, ready to carry his bags to a plush town car.

Me, on the other hand, I'm currently sitting on a crowded train sipping a cup of cold coffee and eating a stale pastry. The only person who is going to be waiting for me when I arrive at the train station in Toulouse is the clerk at the car rental desk. He'll hand me the keys to a compact-size sedan, which I'll use to drive myself to Carcassonne.

The upside of my decidedly less luxurious travel arrangements is that I don't have to sit next to Pierre, look at Pierre, or speak to Pierre.

If I sit next to him, I'm going to be distracted by the smell of his sandalwood and bergamot cologne. Naturally, the smell of Pierre's cologne is going to compel me to glance at his jawline to see if he's freshly shaven or if he has a sexy five o'clock shadow going on.

Once I glance at his jawline, then my gaze will be drawn upward to his hazel eyes. But because his eyes are so mesmerizing, I'll quickly look away, and find myself staring at his suit jacket. I might glimpse one of his cufflinks. I'll probably be momentarily distracted wondering how much they cost, but then my mind will quickly turn to the shirt they're attached to. And we all know that that shirt is hiding broad shoulders, a sculpted chest, a muscular back, and two tattoos. You know exactly what will happen next. To get my mind off of what lies underneath that shirt, I'll start speaking to Pierre.

Speaking? Hah. More like babbling like an idiot. Something along the line of, "How did you get that scar on your back? Do you mind if I see it again? What's the deal with the marmot tattoo? Do you mind if I have another look at it? Can I touch it? It's purely professional interest on my part, I swear."

I shake my head, imagining his reaction to my babbling. His hazel eyes would twinkle, and he'd give me a cocky grin.

See how terribly wrong things could have gone if I had flown on the plane with Pierre? It's a good thing I'm on a crowded train, drinking cold coffee, and eating stale pastry. Better for everyone.

* * *

Pierre pokes his head into the gift shop later that afternoon. "There you are."

I set down the picture I was in the process of hanging, and watch as he walks toward me. Man, he looks so much better wearing a suit than his bellboy uniform.

As he bends down and kisses me on my cheeks, I breathe in the scent of his cologne.

"Do you have a cold?" he asks, offering me the crisp white pocket square from his suit jacket.

"No, why?"

"You're sniffling."

"Sniffling? No, I'm not sniffling. I'm sniffing."

"Sniffing what?"

Realizing how weird it would be to

admit that I was sniffing his neck—that cologne of his is intoxicating—I fake sneeze. "No, you're right, I'm sniffling."

"But you said you were sniffing."

"Don't you think they should make a law against having words sound practically the same? Sniffling with the letter 'l' and 'sniffing' without one. It really makes communication complicated." Then I fake cough.

"Okay, I'm officially confused. Do you have a cold?" He grins. "Or do you have a cod? See what I did there with the missing 'l'?"

I laugh. "I most certainly do not have a fish. But I might be coming down with something."

Yeah, I'm coming down with something for sure. A serious case of falling for a guy who is all wrong for me.

"That's a shame," he says. "I have reservations at Auberge du Canard tonight and I was hoping you would join me."

I pause mid-fake sniffle. Auberge du Canard has won all sorts of awards, been featured on television, and consistently makes the top ten best restaurant lists. Not that any of that matters to me. But what does matter is that if I dine at Auberge du Canard, I can rub it in the faces of everyone at the country club back home.

One of the members—the creepy guy who tried to entice me with an art scholarship—visited southern France last year. Eating at Auberge du Canard was at the top of his list of things to do. But, despite tipping the maître d' an obscene amount of money, he couldn't get a reservation. He was furious. Imagine if I post pictures of me eating there on social media. His head would explode from envy.

"I think it's just allergies," I say.

"Great. Meet you in the lobby at seven."

I try to return his pocket square to him

—I haven't needed it for my fake cold—but he tells me to keep it.

Lightly pressing it against my face, I watch as he chats with the manager of the gift shop about her twin boys. It amazes me how at ease he looks no matter what role he's playing—waiter, bellboy, or hotel executive. Then I wonder what kind of role he's playing with me—flirtatious billionaire or something more serious.

* * *

You know what they say about revenge dining—it's best served bubbling hot. Which is good, as that's exactly how the cassoulet at Auberge du Canard is served.

As the waiter places a rustic, wide-mouthed earthenware bowl on the center of the table, my mouth waters at the smell of the bean stew.

"Cassoulet is traditionally simmered

for four days," Pierre informs me. "Each day, the cook slowly simmers it, then allows it to cool overnight. As it cools, a crust forms on top. The next morning, you pierce the crust, then cook it again. Let it cool overnight, pierce the crust, cool it again, and so on. This allows the beans to absorb the flavors from the meat while retaining their shape."

"Serving a four-old day dish. I wonder if you could get away with that in the States," I muse.

Pierre shakes his head. "This attitude is why fast-food restaurants are so popular in America."

"Hey, I'm not turning my nose up at cassoulet," I say. "No need to be a snob."

"You think I'm a snob?"

I hold up my hands. "No comment."

"If appreciating good food makes me a snob, then I'm happy to be one." Pierre nods at the waiter to serve the cassoulet. As he ladles it onto my plate,

Pierre describes the ingredients. "Those are the finest pork sausages from Toulouse. There are also duck legs, mutton, and of course, white beans. All simmered with rosemary and thyme."

"You forgot the duck confit."

"Ah, I see you already know about cassoulet."

"You can't really go wrong when you cook something with a lot of fat. That's what duck confit is, isn't it?"

"That's true, but French fat is far superior to American fat."

"Says someone who has probably never eaten fries at McDonald's. I'm not sure why we call them French fries, cause they're one hundred percent American. We took potatoes and perfected them."

He grins, then points at my plate. "Go on, try the cassoulet, and then we can compare notes."

First, I take a picture on my phone and post it to my social media accounts, making sure to tag Auberge du Canard and adding the hashtag, "reservations required." Then I groan as I sample the rich, hearty stew. Despite the fact that it's four days old, it's utterly delicious. The beans are soft, the sausages are subtly spiced, the duck is juicy, and the mutton is tender.

Pierre dabs his mouth with a white linen napkin. "Well?"

"It's okay."

"Liar."

"I am not a liar."

"Hmm. Let's see, if I recall correctly, you told me that *Solo* was the best *Star Wars* film. That was clearly a lie. Everyone knows that *Return of the Jedi* is the best one."

"You're delusional," I say before taking another bite of the cassoulet, carefully managing to get a bit of everything onto my fork.

He leans forward, his hazel eyes flickering in the candlelight. "Admit it, you loved the scene when Luke and Leia rode speeder bikes in the forest on Endor."

"Sure," I say between mouthfuls.

"Aha!"

"Aha, nothing." I set my fork down. "Is that why you like marmots so much? Because they look like Ewoks?"

He plucks a piece of crusty baguette from the bread basket. "Hmm . . . I never thought about it that way. I think it's more that I like Ewoks because they remind me of marmots."

"What's the deal with the marmots, anyway? Your family has a hotel named after them and you have a secret tattoo of a marmot on your back."

"Secret being the operative word. There are only a few people who know about my tattoos—you, Amélie, Jean-Paul, Dominic de Santis, and, well, never mind. The important thing is that I want to keep it that way."

I chew a piece of bread thoughtfully.

Who else knows about his tattoos? Who else has seen Pierre without his shirt on? Obviously the person who did his elephant tattoo. When he goes to the gym to work out—and Pierre definitely works out—the guys in the changing room would have seen them. But is there someone else? An old girlfriend, perhaps? Did he get his original elephant tattoo for her? Who is she?

I feel my jaw tightening and it isn't because I'm chewing too hard. The bread isn't that crusty. The thought of another woman seeing Pierre without his shirt on is, well, it's giving me an uncomfortable feeling inside. Something I haven't felt for a long time—jealousy.

"So what's the big deal about having tattoos?" I ask. "You're a grown man. You can do whatever you like. They don't have a stigma like they used to."

Pierre runs his hands through his hair. "It's complicated. Let's just say that my mother would be disappointed."

"It's impossible to go through life without disappointing your mom at some point," I say. "But imagine how much more disappointed she'll be when she finds out about your tattoos and the fact that you didn't tell her about them. Something like that won't stay secret forever."

"I agree," he says. "That's one of the reasons I got the marmot tattoo. When she sees that, she'll—"

I never get to find out what his mother will do because I hear a loud squeal behind me. It's so piercing that I'm surprised the crystal chandelier doesn't crack. I turn, expecting to see a very large guinea pig behind me. Instead, I'm confronted by a woman so stunning that if she isn't already a professional model, it's only because she made a conscious career choice to do voiceover work for documentaries about guinea pigs instead of modeling.

Pierre greets her, kissing one cheek,

then the other. As he goes to pull away, she snakes her perfectly manicured hand through his hair and pulls him toward her, kissing him lightly on the lips. He pulls back, glances at me, and has the decency to look embarrassed.

He introduces us—apparently Pierre went to boarding school with this Giselle chick's brother—then asks who she's dining with.

Giselle points breezily at a large table by the window. I recognize several of the occupants from celebrity magazines. The men look like they played polo earlier, and the women look like they spent the afternoon shopping at exclusive boutiques. "You know, the usual crowd. You should come join us."

"I can't. I'm here with Mia," he says coolly.

I feel my jaw tightening again. *I can't?* That's his response?

Briefly allowing her eyes to graze over me, Giselle responds. "I understand."

I understand? What's that supposed to mean? I feel like there's all sorts of subtext going on here that only someone who has been educated in posh British boarding schools and hangs out with European aristocrats would understand.

She squeezes his arm. "You'll be back in Paris this weekend, right? We're going skydiving on Saturday. You should come. It'll be a blast."

Pierre pauses for a beat, then says, "Mia is afraid of flying."

Now, I'm utterly confused. I'm pretty sure she wasn't inviting *me* skydiving.

Giselle purses her lips for a moment, then gives me a brittle smile. "Such a shame you won't be able to join us." As if dismissing me, she turns to face Pierre. Her fingers trail down his arm. "But we'll see you there, won't we? We haven't done an accelerated free fall together in ages."

The way she says "accelerated free

fall" makes me see red. She's making skydiving sound sexy. How is that even possible?

I drop my fork on my plate, and the noise startles the two of them. "Don't worry, Giselle. I'll be there too. I wouldn't miss it for the world. Jumping out of a plane? Sounds fabulous."

CHAPTER 11
THE COUNTDOWN TIMER

Friday morning rolls around and I'm pacing back and forth in the art gallery at Hôtel de la Marmotte while I periodically check my phone. I've set a timer that is counting down the hours, minutes, and seconds until I have to jump out of a plane. Right now, my appointment with death is twenty-six hours, thirteen minutes, and forty seconds away.

To be fair, that's just a guesstimate. While I know that we have to be at the airport early tomorrow morning, I have no idea how long it's going to take to strap a parachute on, get on the plane, fly up to the right altitude, and then make my leap of doom.

I stop pacing and put my hand to my chest. Jump out of a plane? What was I thinking? I'm too young to die. There's so much I still want to accomplish before my time on this planet is up— open my own combination art gallery and tattoo shop, adopt a cat, and buy a custom-made lightsaber.

My heart flutters, forcing me to acknowledge something I've been trying to suppress. "Be honest with yourself, Mia," it says. "There's one other thing you want to check off your list. You want to kiss Pierre again."

True, heart, so true. Ever since that night at the charity ball when his mother and her poodle interrupted us, we haven't so much as held hands. Initially, that was due to the fact that I had been avoiding Pierre, but things changed for me the night we went to dinner at Auberge du Canard in Carcassonne. After meeting in the lobby of his family's hotel, we strolled through the heart of the picturesque walled city, enjoying the balmy weather.

As we walked through the narrow, winding streets, Pierre regaled me with historical tidbits about the area. But his eyes really lit up when he talked about the local rugby team and how their emblem features an image of the ancient city.

Then our conversation turned to Pierre's charity work. I was surprised when he asked my advice about grassroots fundraising. He told me that he felt uneasy about hosting extravagant fundraisers, especially when a significant portion of the money raised went to putting on the fundraiser itself, rather than to the orphanages. I wondered if I had misjudged him.

Maybe you could be insanely wealthy and still be a good guy.

When I stumbled on the cobblestones, Pierre briefly grabbed my elbow and steadied me. Then he abruptly dropped his hand. At the time, I chalked it up to him knowing that I didn't approve of public displays of affection.

When we were at the restaurant and he reached across the table, I thought he was going to squeeze my hand. Turns out he just wanted some salt for his appetizer of wild mushrooms sautéed in fresh herbs.

By the time our cassoulet arrived, I was itching for him to touch me, even if it was to casually brush his fingers against mine. Then, of course, you know what happened—Giselle arrived on the scene, reminding me of Pierre's true nature. A spoiled billionaire who was out on some sort of pity date with me. The rest of the evening was awkward, the conversation was stilted, and I was glad when it was over.

But still, I wanted to kiss him. And I still do. What does that say about me? That I don't care that Pierre is a rich jerk? That I care about Pierre despite the fact that he's a rich jerk? Or that I just want to put Giselle in her place?

Truthfully, it's probably the latter. Girls like Giselle deserve to know that just because you look like a supermodel doesn't mean you can have everything you want.

My heart flutters, then softly says, "Are you sure you're being honest with yourself, Mia? Is this really about Giselle? Or is this about protecting yourself?"

* * *

Twenty-one hours, twelve minutes, and two seconds until things go splat on the ground. Things being me. I need to know more about what I'm getting myself into.

I ask Amélie if I can take a break. She says yes, provided that I return with an espresso for her and a chocolate croissant for me. She's getting tired of my pacing back and forth and the constant checking of my phone. She's hoping a sugar buzz will soothe my frazzled nerves. I'm not sure she understands how sugar works on the nervous system, but a croissant does sound good.

As I walk toward the concierge desk, I pause to watch the daily parade of ducks. Bellboys, waiters, and desk clerks make a procession down the grand staircase to the large reflection pool in the center of the lobby. Each of them carries a yellow rubber ducky nestled on a small red velvet cushion. With great ceremony, they lower their ducks into the water, carefully holding onto them so that they can't drift away. Then the front desk manager strikes a gong. All the hotel guests wait in hushed anticipation while the lights on the bottom of the pool are illuminated and the fountain in the center of the pool starts to bubble. The hotel manager strikes his gong a second time, and the ducks are released to float aimlessly around the pool. Everyone applauds, chattering among themselves about how delightfully quirky Hôtel de la Marmotte is.

Pierre catches my eye as he hands his velvet cushion to a fellow bellboy. He starts to walk toward me, but his mother calls his name. Giving me an apologetic look, he turns and follows her into her office.

I watch the duckies for a few moments, trying to reconcile the odd touches at the hotel, such as the duck parade and the oil painting of a marmot on a Harley Davidson at the entrance to the restaurant, with Pierre's mother. She seems so formal, so aloof, so serious, so not fun. Yet, according to Pierre, this hotel is her baby. She purchased the building, oversaw the renovation, and turned it into one of the hottest boutique hotels in Paris, if not in all of Europe.

I shrug and continue on my way. The woman hasn't said one single solitary word to me since I started working here. It's not like we're suddenly going to become best friends and she's going to spill all her hotelier secrets to me. Everything about the Hôtel de la Marmotte is probably a dry, commercial decision on her part, carefully calculated to attract more guests and bring in more money to the Toussaint empire.

When I reach the concierge desk, Jean-Paul nods at me. While he assists a woman with tickets to the Moulin Rouge, I pick up a skydiving brochure from a rack by the hotel entrance. The pictures on the front, of people smiling while they're hurtling toward the ground, would lead you to believe that jumping out of a plane from ten thousand feet in the air is the ultimate thrill.

It's not like I read the dictionary regularly, but I'm pretty sure that the word "thrill" means a feeling of excitement and pleasure. Obviously, whoever designed this brochure has no clue about the English language. Skydiving isn't thrilling; it's terrifying. I grab a pen from the desk, cross out "ultimate thrill" and replace it with "ultimate terror." Truth in advertising is important.

"What are you doing, Mia?" Jean-Paul asks. When I show him the brochure, he smiles. "I heard you're going skydiving. I have to say that I was surprised. I thought you were afraid of flying."

"I am."

He cocks his head to one side. "I don't understand."

"Yeah, that makes two of us." I fiddle with the brochure in my hand. "What do you know about this Giselle chick?"

"Ah, now I think I understand," Jean-Paul says. "Pierre told me that Giselle was at Auberge du Canard when the two of you were there. She is very fond of skydiving. I suppose she'll be there tomorrow?"

I nod, picturing Giselle looking like a James Bond girl in a form-fitting jumpsuit, the zipper pulled down to expose a lacy bra, high-heeled boots, and designer goggles perched on her head. She'll fawn all over Pierre, then the two of them will gracefully jump out of the plane. After performing acrobatic maneuvers in the air, they'll glide to the ground, land effortlessly, then embrace passionately.

"Did the two of them used to date?" I blurt out.

"You don't need to worry about Giselle," Jean-Paul says.

"Who says I'm worried?"

He points at the brochure I'm holding. I seem to have torn it into tiny pieces.

Half of them are still clenched in my hand. The other half are scattered on the desk. "You're clearly anxious about something."

"I'm worried about dying."

"Skydiving is perfectly safe," Jean-Paul says.

"But what if I forget to pull the parachute in time? What if the cord breaks? What if my parachute has a giant tear in it? What if—"

Jean-Paul holds up his hand. "You don't need to worry about any of that. For your first skydive, you'll be doing a tandem."

"A what?"

"A tandem. You'll be harnessed to someone else. All you'll have to do is enjoy the ride down."

"Harnessed to someone else? That sounds weird."

Jean-Paul pulls another brochure off the rack and opens it up. "See how this woman is wearing a full-body harness?

It's connected to her instructor's harness. He has the parachute on his back."

"What if the instructor forgets to deploy the parachute?"

"Pierre won't forget. He's very experienced."

"Pierre?"

"Yes, he's planning on doing the tandem dive with you. He's a certified skydiving instructor."

Well, of course he is. In addition to running a charity for African orphanages, working as a bellboy, and filling in for his father at meetings, he also teaches people about how to hurtle themselves to death from a plane. Next, I'll find out that he also does brain surgery in his spare time.

Jean-Paul pats my hand. "I probably shouldn't tell you this, but I've never seen Pierre like this with any girl before."

"Like what?"

"Like . . ." He scratches his head, trying to think of the word in English. "Smitten. Yes, that's what it is. He's smitten with you."

I smile. Smitten is such an old-fashioned term. Cute, but old-fashioned. Then my expression sobers. "I doubt that Pierre is smitten with me."

"No, he definitely is," Jean-Paul says. "I know that he met with his lawyer yesterday to discuss a matter related to you."

My stomach clenches. "His lawyer? Why in the world would he do that?"

"I've said too much." Jean-Paul shakes his head. "It's best if Pierre explains the rest."

He refuses to divulge any more information, no matter how persistently I question him. Eventually, I give up.

After walking over to the cafe and ordering an espresso for Amélie, I glance at my phone. Nineteen hours, thirty-two minutes, and twenty seconds until I do a tandem skydive with Pierre. I've never been more terrified in my life.

* * *

It's Saturday morning. Four hours, two minutes, and thirty-six seconds to go, and I still haven't come up with a way to get out of skydiving.

While I wait outside the hotel for Pierre to pick me up, I think about my options. My best idea so far has been to buy a life-size dummy—like the ones they use in automobile crash tests—dress it up like me, sneak it aboard the plane, strap a parachute on it, then jettison it once we reach the jump altitude. But when I talked it over with Isabelle, she pointed out a few flaws with my plan.

First, a crash test dummy can't pull a ripcord. When no one sees the parachute unfurl, they'll assume the worst. An ambulance will race over, sirens blaring, expecting to find my dead body. Instead, they'll see the dummy's head with a blonde wig on it, and plastic arms and legs scattered about.

Second, Pierre and I are supposed to tandem skydive. Do I really think he won't notice when a crash test dummy is strapped to him instead of me? We've been up close and personal before, kissing at the charity ball. He's bound to notice that something isn't quite right. And, if he can't spot the difference between me and a plastic mannequin, I have bigger problems than jumping out of a plane.

Third, crash dummies don't come cheap. My credit card is already maxed out. I can barely afford to buy an espresso, let alone make a purchase that large.

I tap my foot anxiously while I wait for Pierre's car to pull up. *Think, Mia, think. There has to be a way to get out of this.*

Fake an illness? No, Pierre would probably see through that one. I've already told him how I used to pretend to have a stomachache when I wanted to get out of selling Girl Scout cookies door-to-door. I loved being a Girl Scout. Selling cookies, not so much.

My phone informs me that the hours, minutes, and seconds are ticking away. Do I have enough time to get a coffee before Pierre gets here? More importantly, do I have enough money? I rummage in my backpack, but only find sixty-five cents. That's definitely not enough. And we all know that my credit card—

Hey, wait a minute. That's it! How come I didn't think of this before? Skydiving costs hundreds of euros. When I go to pay for it, my credit card is going to be declined. The perfect reason to bow out of jumping out of a plane. Sure, Giselle and all her snooty friends will snicker about how poor I am, but isn't it better to be poor than dead?

Pierre pulls up in the circular

driveway in front of the hotel. He's driving a sleek sports car today, instead of being chauffeured around in a town car. A valet opens the passenger door for me and I slip in.

"Sorry I'm late," Pierre says. "I've been on a conference call all morning. And I have a few more calls to make on the way to the airport." Then he hands me a steaming cup of coffee, his fingers brushing against mine. "I thought you might need this. When you texted this morning, you said that you didn't sleep well. Nerves?"

I picture Giselle, the skydiving daredevil supermodel in my head, and lie. "No, not at all."

"Really? You're afraid of flying. You know, you can always change your mind. No one will think less of you."

"Honestly, I'll be fine. The fear of flying is probably an advantage. I'll want to get off the plane so badly that I'll happily jump out of it."

He rubs his jaw. "Wow, I'm amazed at how brave you are."

I smile brightly at him. It's easy to be brave when you know that your credit card is going to be declined. Once that transaction doesn't go through, I'm home free.

On the ride to the small airport in the north of France where the skydiving operation is located, I take in the scenery while Pierre makes several business-related calls. His father seems to be involving him more in the day-to-day management of the family's commercial empire. I wonder if his parents are going to put an end to his rotation through front-line hotel jobs and promote him to an executive position early.

I glance over at Pierre and frown. The stubble on his chin and the dark circles under his eyes are signs that he's burning the candle at both ends of the stick. When he stops at an intersection, he stretches his arms above his head and yawns, before taking another call. This time it's to his lawyer, who he agrees to meet briefly at the airport to go through some important papers.

I shake my head. Only billionaires have their lawyers come running to them, fitting in business deals around skydiving, polo, and charity balls. The rest of us make appointments and wait patiently in the reception area until the lawyer has time to see us. And when we deal with lawyers, it's usually for some unpleasant reason, like the reading of a will or a divorce, not because we're brokering some multi-million dollar property acquisition or company merger.

When we arrive at the airport, we're greeted by Giselle. She squeals loudly when she sees Pierre. I roll my eyes as she attempts to lock lips with him again. Despite her efforts, Pierre simply gives her a couple of brief air kisses, then steps back and puts his arm around my shoulders. For once, I'm not upset about a public display of affection. The look on Giselle's face is totally worth it.

"You remember Mia, don't you?" Pierre asks.

Giselle gives an indifferent nod in my direction, then points at a group of people standing by a sign that says, *Skydive Beaumont*. "Everyone's here. Come, say hello."

Pierre squeezes my shoulder before he leads me over. There's a lot of kissing of cheeks, gossip about a rumored royal abdication, arrangements for a birthday party on a private island in the Caribbean, and plans to go to a nightclub later that night.

I stand awkwardly to the side, wondering if this group of self-absorbed people would have even noticed if a crash test dummy was standing here instead of me.

After a few minutes, a man with an uncanny resemblance to Bruce Willis takes pity on me. "You're, Mia, right? I'm Stefan, owner of Skydive Beaumont. Pierre told me that this will be your first time skydiving. You're our only beginner today, so while everyone else has some coffee, I'm going to take you through a short orientation session."

I pull my wallet out of my purse. For once in my life, I'm glad my credit rating sucks. Not that I actually knew what a credit rating was until Isabelle explained it to me a few weeks ago. "Uh, sure, but first I need to pay for it."

Stefan shakes his head. "No need to worry about that. Pierre's taken care of everything. It's his treat. The only thing you have to concern yourself with is jumping out of the plane."

CHAPTER 12
ALL THE SHADES OF GREEN

Thirty-two minutes, five seconds later, I walk out of Stefan's office. I've watched a video about skydiving, produced a medical certificate, signed release papers, and quickly done a search on my phone to see if I can get a rush delivery of a crash test dummy to the airport.

"Are you okay?" Giselle asks. This is the most she's said to me since we've met, so I'm immediately suspicious.

"Yes, why?"

"Well, you do look a bit green." She waves her friends over. "Girls, take a look at Mia. Doesn't her complexion look green? I think she's using the wrong foundation."

The girls pepper me with questions while inspecting my skin. "Do you use primer?" "What kind of moisturizer are you using?" "Are your pores always this large?"

Then a fervent discussion breaks out about what a massive job doing a makeover on me would entail. A twenty-four carat gold facial enriched with Mongolian yak butter is mentioned. Someone suggests that Botox needs to be seriously considered. A Russian reality show star scoffs at the Botox idea. Apparently that isn't enough to deal with the tragic mess that is my face. "Sweetheart," she says in a husky voice, "I give you name of plastic surgeon. He do good job on you."

Meanwhile, Pierre, Stefan and the

other guys are standing by the coffee station chatting about rugby. While normally I wouldn't gravitate toward a discussion about conversion kicks, it has to be better than listening to these girls.

I slip away unnoticed—they've moved on from discussing my facial shortcomings and are now talking about the new rutabaga diet fad—and sit on a couch next to the coffee station. Listening with half an ear to the guys, I leaf through a celebrity magazine. I do a double take when I realize that the woman on the cover is the same one who recommended plastic surgery to me.

Pierre turns to refill his coffee cup. I start to say hi to him, but Stefan comes over and slaps him on the back. "I hear wedding bells are on the horizon."

Pierre glances over at where the girls are standing and shushes him. "It's meant to be a surprise."

"Relax, they can't hear you," Stefan says. "From what you tell me though, I think she's going to be shocked. A proposal so soon after meeting? But I suppose with a diamond that big, she's hardly going to say no."

I burrow into the couch and hide behind my magazine. I don't think Pierre and Stefan realize that they've been overheard. My mind is whirring. Who is going to propose to whom? Then I stifle a giggle when I realize that I've said "whom" with a British accent. Granted, I said it inside my mind, not out loud, but I'd never normally talk like that. I'd say, "Who is going to propose to who?" And I'd say it with my flat, American accent.

The pilot walks into the reception area. "We're ready to take you up. Grab your gear and head over to the plane."

Pierre grabs Stefan's arm. "My lawyer was supposed to be here by now, and I really need to see him today. Can you give me a few minutes? I'll give him a call and see where he's at."

"Oh, yeah. That's part of the surprise you have planned, right?" Stefan waves the pilot over, then turns back to Pierre. "No problem. I'll take care of it."

As Pierre pulls out his phone, a harried-looking man rushes in. Oblivious to my presence, the two of them confer in hushed tones, while the lawyer sets his briefcase down next to the coffeemaker. He opens it, pulls out a stack of file folders, and shuffles through them. Pierre frowns and taps his fingers on the table. The lawyer mutters to himself while he looks through his briefcase again. Finally, he finds the right folder, and hands it to Pierre, along with a fountain pen. Pierre flips through the document, then signs his name on the last page with a flourish.

After he hands it back to the lawyer, Pierre rushes out of the reception area toward the airplane. I consider my options—do I stay here and continue to read my magazine, or do I join the others on the plane? Except for the discussion of my face, I've gone pretty much unnoticed by everyone. They might not even realize that I haven't boarded.

But, on the other hand, something is going on with Pierre, and I'm curious to find out what this urgent meeting with the lawyer was really about.

Nosiness wins out. As I stand and go to set the magazine on the table, the lawyer turns and bumps into me. His briefcase tumbles to the ground, and the file folders and papers fly out. I bend down to help him retrieve them. The documents all seem pretty dry and boring, full of lawyerly stuff. That is, until I get to one with the heading, "Accord Prénuptial." My online French refresher course has really been paying off because I know that this translates to "Prenuptial Agreement."

The lawyer snatches it from my hand

and sticks it in a folder labeled, "Toussaint." Toussaint as in Pierre Toussaint.

Whoa, wait a minute. Why is Pierre signing a prenuptial agreement? Is he going to pull a diamond engagement ring out of the pocket of his jumpsuit and propose to Giselle on board the plane? Stefan mentioned that there were wedding bells in the air. I knew there was something weird going on between Pierre and Giselle. They must have had a fight and broken up. I bet he was only using me to make her jealous. He knew she would be at Auberge du Canard that night. That's why he asked me to go to dinner with him, so that she'd see him with another woman. He played it cool when Giselle showed up, but it was all for show. He's in love with her. He's always been in love with her. And now he's going to ask her to be his wife.

The pilot walks into the reception area.

"Mia, we're waiting for you."

"Just give me a few minutes." I go into the ladies' room and splash cold water on my face. After taking a few deep breaths, I look at myself in the mirror. Wow, my complexion really does look green. But is it green from the anxiety of having to jump out of a plane, or is it green from envy?

My phone beeps. The timer reads zero. Turns out the countdown wasn't for the hours, minutes and seconds until I went skydiving. It was to count down the time until my heart was broken.

* * *

"There you are," Pierre says as I board the plane. "I was beginning to think you were going to stand me up."

Around a dozen people are seated on jump seats arranged against the sides of the aircraft. Like me, they're all wearing jumpsuits, helmets, and goggles. Unlike me, they all look thrilled to be here. Giselle especially. Little does she know her day is about to get even better.

Pierre taps the empty seat next to him. "I saved you a spot."

I gulp as I fasten my seatbelt. "I can't go through with this."

Pierre squeezes my hand. "It's okay, you can do this. Think of it like that scene on the Death Star when Stormtroopers are shooting at Luke and Leia and they have to do that Tarzan-like swing across that giant chasm."

"Are you saying people are going to be shooting at us when we jump out of the airplane?"

He laughs. "No, there won't be any shooting."

"Are we going to be swinging on vines?"

"Nope, no vines."

"And Planet Earth isn't in danger of being destroyed by a Death Star?"

"Not that I'm aware of."

"Then why are you bringing up *Star Wars*?"

He pinches my nose playfully. "Because I thought it would distract you from the fact that the plane is about to take off."

Giselle leans across the aisle. "If she doesn't want to do it, don't make her."

"I'm not making her do anything," Pierre says. "Mia knows that."

Giselle shakes her head. "Look at her. She's turning green again."

Pierre puts his finger under my chin and tips my face up. "You do look a little green."

"Must be all that pea soup I had earlier. I'm totally on board with jumping out of this plane. But I don't feel right that you paid for it."

"Is that what's bothering you?" He adjusts his goggles. "Don't be silly. It's my pleasure."

"Remember the first time we went

skydiving, Pierre?" Giselle asks. "It was right after you came back from your gap year in Africa."

The discussion of their first skydiving adventure leaves me puzzled. I'd scratch my head if I wasn't wearing a helmet. Let's see, Stefan said that the girl Pierre was going to propose to would be surprised because they had only known each other for a short time. But Pierre went to boarding school with Giselle's brother. That means he's known her for ages. So it can't be Giselle who he's going to ask to marry him. But if it isn't Giselle, who does he want to be his bride?

Pierre smiles at me in a way that gives me butterflies in my stomach. Or maybe not. It could just be nerves making my tummy queasy. He leans in and whispers in my ear, "I have a surprise for you when we land."

My eyes widen. A surprise? Hang on. I've only known Pierre for a short time.

Is it *me* he's going to propose to?

"Wow, I didn't think it was possible to turn any greener," Giselle says as the plane taxis to the runway.

The engines rumble, and I feel a vibration as we speed up for takeoff. As the plane lifts off the ground, I clutch my stomach.

"Don't worry, Mia," Pierre says. "I'll take care of you."

Take care of me? I narrow my eyes. I don't need to be taken care of. This is exactly the way my ex treated me. Like a china doll he had to protect. Like a little girl he had to help learn how to walk. Like a charity case he had to assist by paying for everything.

I'm so angry that I barely notice we're in the air. It isn't until I glance out the window and see clouds that I realize I'm flying in an airplane.

Pierre taps me on the shoulder. "Come on, let's double check your harness."

After making sure everything is securely connected, Pierre and I walk toward the airplane door. By this point, I'm ready to jump. The sooner this ordeal is over with, the better. All I want to do is get to the ground as quickly as possible, then escape from this French billionaire before he proposes.

"Ready?" Pierre asks.

As we step off the plane, I yell, "There's no way I'd ever get married again, especially not to you!"

* * *

This is terrifying! No, this is exhilarating! Terrifying! Exhilarating! It's a terrifying exhilaration!

Can you tell that I don't have a clue what I'm feeling as Pierre and I plummet toward certain death? Stefan told me that I'd experience thirty seconds of free-fall before Pierre pulls the ripcord and deploys the parachute. But this feels like it's been going on for way longer than half a minute.

I scream as we continue to free-fall. Something must have happened. Is the parachute broken? Did Pierre lose consciousness? We're going to die.

"But at least you'll die in Pierre's arms," a tiny voice whispers. "It's so romantic."

That must be my heart speaking. The only thing my stomach has been saying since we jumped out of the plane is, "I'm going to throw up."

"Seriously, heart, zip it," I say. "There's nothing romantic about dying in someone's arms. This isn't *Romeo and Juliet*."

Before my heart can argue with me, I feel the parachute deploying. Our speed decreases dramatically. We're gently soaring through the air like birds. It's actually a pleasant feeling, slowly gliding down toward the ground. When we near our landing site, I remember

Stefan's instructions and lift my legs. I feel a huge grin spread across my face as Pierre and I slide onto the ground. I survived!

Someone from Skydive Beaumont rushes over and unhooks the parachute and our harnesses.

Pierre unstraps his helmet and places it in the crook of his arm. He steps toward me, his lips pressed tightly together. After a beat, he asks, "Are you okay?"

I glance down. All my limbs still seem to be attached to my body. I don't see any blood. I have a ringing in my ears, but that's probably from all the screaming I did on the way down. All in all, I probably fared better than a crash test dummy would have.

"I'm okay."

His eyes turn steely. Tossing his helmet on the ground, he grabs me by my arms and pulls me toward him. For a moment, I think he's going to kiss me.

Then I realize that's the furthest thing from his mind. "Why didn't you tell me you had been married before?" he asks, the tone in his voice icy.

I pull away from him and take a step back. "Because it was none of your business, that's why."

"It's very much my business."

"Your business?" I clench my fists. "Are you delusional? Just because your family owns half of France doesn't mean you're entitled to know everything. To have everything you want. To have everyone you want."

He folds his arms across his chest. "My family does not own half of France. Much of our holdings are overseas."

"Seriously, that's the part of this conversation you're focusing on?"

"It's the only semi-rational thing you've said." He paces for a few moments, then points back and forth between the two us. "I thought we had something here. I thought you understood me. I thought you saw beyond my family's wealth. But, no, you assume that just because I was lucky enough to be born into money, that I'm a jerk."

"I've known a lot of guys like you," I say. "Maybe they're not as rich as you are, but they're rich enough, and each and every single one has been a jerk."

Pierre's shoulders slump. "Is that what you really think of me?"

"I don't know what to think anymore, to be honest." I chew on my lip. "When I first met you, you were a waiter. I thought you were just a normal guy, trying to make a living. I liked you. We had fun together. Then I got to Paris and discovered that you're not just some ordinary guy, you're the heir to the Toussaint fortune. And that's when things changed."

"How did things change? I was the same guy you met on the cruise ship."

I put my hands on my hips. "No, you weren't. You tried to buy me off. You tried to control me. The free room at the hotel. The job at the art gallery. You wanted to prove how much better you were than me. How little old me from Small Town, USA could never survive in Paris without you."

"If that's what you thought, why did you accept my help?"

I'm at a loss for words. Why did I accept his help? I didn't want to. Isabelle, Ginny, and Celeste all convinced me that I was reading too much into everything. That he was just being nice. That he was just being my friend. Was that why I said yes to his assistance?

When I don't respond, he mutters, "She was right. You're a gold digger, just like the rest of them."

"She? Who? Your mother?"

Pierre furrows his brow. "My mother?"

"I've seen how she looks at me. Like I'm something you find on your shoe. Like I'm beneath her."

"You don't know my mother very well," he says.

"I know enough. I've dealt with women like her before. They don't want their sons to marry girls from the wrong side of the tracks. My mother-in-law was just like her."

"Your mother-in-law. Yeah, let's get back to the original topic. Why didn't you tell me you were married before? Was that because you ran out on your husband? Did you abandon him?" He narrows his eyes. "Who else did you abandon?"

I throw my hands up in the air. "I didn't abandon anyone."

"Sure. And why should I believe you?" He starts to walk away from me, then doubles back. Jabbing his finger into my chest, he says, "I'm glad I found out about the real you before it was too late."

"You mean before you asked me to marry you?"

"Marry you? Talk about delusional. Why do you think I wanted to marry you?"

"Stefan mentioned something about wedding bells. I saw the prenuptial agreement your lawyer brought to the airport for you to sign."

He arches an eyebrow. "A prenuptial? Trust me, that's not what he was there to discuss with me. You do realize that lawyers have more than one client, don't you? Honestly, did you really think I was going to propose to you? That talk about wedding bells had to do with a friend of ours who is going to propose to his girlfriend. It had absolutely nothing to do with you. Nothing."

I feel my face grow warm. The lawyer was flustered when he was picking up the papers. He probably put the prenuptial agreement back into the wrong folder. It didn't have anything to do with Pierre. How could I have been so stupid?

"What he brought for me to look at was something entirely different." Pierre gives me a scathing look. "Something that's completely irrelevant now."

As he strides away from me, I feel my chest tightening. Unzipping the top of my jumpsuit so that I can breathe, I think about what's happened today. I don't think I'm afraid of flying anymore, but I am afraid of something far worse— losing Pierre.

CHAPTER 13
GOING BLUE

After Pierre storms off, Stefan graciously offers to drive me back to the hotel. The ride back is quiet. At first, Stefan tries to engage me in conversation, but when my responses continue to consist of one-word answers, he gives up.

I go to my suite at the hotel and pack my bags. I have no idea where I'm going to sleep tonight, but I know it won't be here. I'm tempted to tuck a few bottles of the begonia-scented shampoo and conditioner in my purse, but I resist.

I don't want to be beholden to Pierre any longer, not even for floral-scented hair.

Gathering up the last of my personal belongings, I take one last look at my home for the past few months. The large claw-foot bathtub, the comfortable king-size bed, the marmot painting over the fireplace, and the Louis the Sixteenth furniture in the living room all try to tempt me to stay. I need to get out of here quickly before I succumb to temptation. I've gotten way too accustomed to living in luxurious surroundings. This isn't who I am. I'm a simple girl, used to sleeping on a futon in a studio apartment.

I scoot out the door before I change my mind. It makes an oddly satisfying clicking noise as it closes behind me. The sound of something ending. Something that never should have started.

Once I'm in the elevator, I take a deep

breath. The next thing I'm planning to do is going to be much harder. I have to tell Amélie that I can't work at the art gallery anymore.

As I walk through the lobby, I smile at the rubber duckies floating in the reflecting pool. Visions of Pierre carrying a velvet pillow as part of the daily duck parade flash through my head. He looked so goofy in that bellboy uniform of his, but it didn't seem to faze him. He seemed genuinely happy to wear it, performing the most mundane tasks for hotel guests. To look at him, you'd never realize that his family owned the hotel. He was at ease with all the rest of the staff, making them feel like he was just one of the gang.

Shaking my head, I push open the door to the art gallery. Amélie is at the sales counter with some customers. She raises her eyebrows when she sees my bags and motions for me to wait. While she rings up their purchase,

I stroll around looking at the artwork on display. There's a new collection of miniature paintings in the corner—each one depicting a field mouse next to a different kind of flower. It's the type of thing my mom would love. I snap a photo with my phone. Considering how much they're selling for, it's the closest she's going to get to having one.

"What's going on?" Amélie says after she escorts the customers out of the gallery. "Why do you have your bags?"

"I'm leaving Hôtel de la Marmotte," I say.

"Oh, have you found an apartment?" She knows that I've been looking for one in what little spare time I've had. But finding something halfway decent in my price range had been a challenge, and Pierre kept insisting it wasn't a problem for me to stay at the hotel, so my search had been half-hearted at best.

"Not exactly." I feel my eyes welling

up, and I pull a tissue out of my purse.

"Then why are you leaving?"

I dab my eyes and sniffle. "Because I have to."

Amélie leads me over to the seating area by the window, then walks briskly to the door and flips the sign from "ouvert" to "fermé."

"No, you can't close the gallery on my account," I protest.

"Nonsense. You're upset." She sits next to me and pats my knee. "Tell me what's happened."

I spill my guts, telling her how I had mistakenly thought Pierre was going to propose to me. "I made a fool out of myself."

"No, not a fool, *cherié*. It is not foolish to be in love."

"But, I'm not in love."

She smiles gently at me. "Are you sure about that?"

"Absolutely. I could never love Pierre and . . ." I crumple up the tissue in my hand as my voice trails off.

"And what?"

I walk over to the trash can and throw the tissue away. Turning back to Amélie, I say firmly, "And Pierre could never love me."

Amélie stands and smooths down her skirt. She looks as elegant as ever—the epitome of a chic Parisian woman. I'm still wearing my skydiving jumpsuit, my hair is a tangled mess, and one of my sneakers is untied. The contrast between the two of us couldn't be starker.

This is just one of the many reasons why Pierre and I aren't suited for each other. I lack the poise and fashion sense that women like Amélie, Giselle, and Pierre's mother have. Pierre needs someone who he can proudly display on his arm at charity balls.

"Now, I suppose the next thing you were planning on telling me is that you can't work here anymore." When I start to protest, she says, "Let me speak. I have seen girls like you before. Girls who don't believe in themselves."

"That's not true. I believe in myself."

"You think the only reason you got this job is because Pierre told me to hire you, *non*?" When I nod my head, she says, "You are wrong. I *considered* you for the job because Pierre sent me your resume and suggested that you might be a good fit."

I spread my hands. "Exactly."

"But it is I," Amélie taps her chest, "*moi*, who hired you, not Pierre. I am the one who read your articles in *Art Girl Moderne* and recognized how knowledgeable you were about art. I am the one who spoke with the gentleman you did your apprenticeship with."

"You talked to Henry Tusk?"

"He spoke very highly about your dedication and eagerness to learn. I also spoke with your manager at the last tattoo parlor you were employed at. He told me what a hard worker you are. You always went above and beyond what was required. Both of them also mentioned something which is very important to me—your artistic talent."

Staring at the marble floor, I feel overwhelmed by what Amélie has said. "They think I'm talented?" I ask softly.

"Yes, *cherié*. So, now you understand why I hired you? Not because of Pierre. And I made a good decision, *non*? You work hard, you are good with customers, and you have done an excellent job organizing the tattoo photography exhibition. So, you will continue to work for me."

When I raise my eyes, Amélie is giving me a look that reminds me of my second-grade teacher, Mrs. Murphy. "*Oui, madame.* I'll continue to work here."

"But I do think you need some time away from all this." Amélie waves her arms around the gallery. "Take a few days off." She pulls her purse out from underneath the counter and hands me a set of keys. "You can stay with Jean-Paul and me."

"But, I can't," I say. "What about the exhibition? We have so much to do to be ready on time."

She tucks a strand of my hair behind my ear and makes soothing noises. I nearly break down at the gesture. It reminds me of how my mother would comfort me when I was upset. "Mia, everything will be fine with the exhibition. You've worked so hard on it. There isn't anything else that needs to be done that I or someone else can't handle."

"But I want it to be perfect," I say.

"It will be," she reassures me. After writing down the address to her and Jean-Paul's apartment, she ushers me out the door.

* * *

After I arrive at Amélie and Jean-Paul's, I instantly feel some of my stress melt away. As stunning as the suite at Hôtel de la Marmotte was, I prefer the homeyness of this apartment. The decor is stylish, but it's also comfortable. Deep couches you want to sink into, leather armchairs next to a cozy fireplace, and a large dining table that looks like it has been in the family for generations.

I set my bags down in the guest room, then lie on the bed. I didn't sleep a wink the previous night because I kept tossing, turning, and staring at the skydiving countdown timer on my phone. A nap would do me good, but I'm not sure I'll be able to fall asleep. Thoughts of how angry Pierre was with me keep flashing in my head. So what if he didn't know I had been married before? It's not like he didn't keep plenty of secrets from me either. In fact, there are still things I don't know about him, like how he got that scar on his back, what his relationship with Giselle is, and why he's obsessed with marmots.

I feel my eyes grow heavy. Turning on my side, I pull a blanket over me and drift off to sleep. At least I think I'm falling asleep. Maybe I'm already asleep. I really hope this all is just a bad dream. I pray that when I wake up, I'll find myself on my futon in my old apartment back home.

* * *

"Wake up, *cherié*." I feel someone tap my shoulder. "Mia, we're going to have dinner soon. Time to get up."

I rub my eyes. This can't be my apartment. Instead of framed *Star Wars* posters on the walls, there's floral wallpaper. And this isn't a futon I'm lying on. It's a queen-size bed with a wrought iron headboard. The white chest of drawers looks antique, not like it came from a flat pack. Where am I?

"*Cherié*, are you okay?"

I sit up, propping a pillow behind my back. Someone just called me *cherié*. I know exactly where I am—Paris. It wasn't a dream. It all happened. From meeting Pierre on the cruise ship, getting a job at the art gallery, staying at the suite at Hôtel Marmot, going to a fancy charity ball, kissing Pierre, to jumping out of a plane with him.

I run my hands through the snarls in my hair, then smile faintly at Amélie. "I'm okay. Nothing a shower wouldn't help."

She opens up an armoire and hands me a stack of fluffy towels. "The bathroom is down the hall. Come join us when you're ready. We'll have an apéritif, then I thought you might want to help us make dinner. I remember you saying how much you wanted to learn how to cook steak frites properly."

I open my suitcase to pull out my toiletry bag. Lying next to it is a plastic bag. Ooh, I forgot I had bought hair dye. Time to say goodbye to the old Mia and hello to a new and improved Mia.

After mixing up the solution, applying it to my hair, and wrapping it in a plastic cap, I perch on the edge of the bathtub and check my phone. Pierre hasn't called or texted. No surprise there. I don't expect I'll ever be hearing from him again. I do have a cryptic voicemail from Celeste, though.

I dial her number, hoping her message doesn't mean what I think it means.

When she answers the phone, she sounds chirpy, but I have no idea what she's saying.

"That's how you say hello in Greek, dear," she explains.

"It sounds like a really hard language to pronounce," I say. "The only thing I can say in Greek is 'baklava.'"

"That's a good start," Celeste says. "My niece, Olivia, makes wonderful baklava. She had a great teacher. I

SMITTEN WITH CROISSANTS   281

think I told you about Xander, didn't I?"

"The guy that owns the taverna on the island where you're staying?"

"Uh-huh. He showed her his family's secret baklava recipe. I know you rave about the croissants in Paris, but seriously, the baklava here is to die for. Honey-soaked pastry with nuts. Absolutely delicious. Ginny had some when she was here. She loved it."

"Maybe someday I'll get to Greece," I say. "But right now, I have a lot going on in Paris."

"And how is Pierre?"

"Hang on a minute." I set the phone down and check my hair. A little bit of dye is dripping down my neck. After dabbing it off with a tissue, I pick the phone back up. "Remember the photography exhibition I was telling you about? The opening night is next week. Tons to do for it."

"That's nice, dear, but I didn't ask you about work. I asked you about Pierre."

"Um, well, honestly, things aren't great."

"Don't tell me you broke up."

"Broke up? That's a good question. It's not like we were seriously dating. Can you break up with someone if you've only been out with them a few times?" Then I furrow my brow. Exactly how many times did Pierre and I go out? Was it a few times or less than that? I press the phone to my head with my shoulder while I count on my fingers.

First, there was the *Star Wars* convention. I'm not sure that qualifies as a date. It might have simply been two friends attending an event where they can geek out over spaceships, lightsabers, and alien life forms. I suspect that the people Pierre normally hangs out with aren't sci-fi fans.

Second, there was the charity ball. That had to have been our first official date. I'm not the kind of girl to drag a guy out to a patio and make-out with him unless we're dating.

Third up was the dinner at Auberge du Canard. Was that a date? Or was that just a dinner between two colleagues who happened to be in the same city at the same time for work? Giselle's sudden appearance at the restaurant and Pierre's reaction to her makes it hard to categorize that one.

When I get to my ring finger, I sigh. The fourth pseudo-date Pierre and I had was today when we went skydiving. And we all know how that ended.

"Earth to Mia," Celeste says. "Something's obviously happened between the two of you."

"It did," I say simply. "And I promise to tell you all about it later. But right now, I have to go wash my hair."

Celeste hums a familiar-sounding show tune, then chuckles. "Are you going to wash that man right out of your hair too?"

"Uh, no. Just hair dye."

"Sometimes, I forget how young you are. I don't suppose you ever saw *South Pacific*. One day, I'll have to tell you about the time I was in an off-Broadway production of it. Anyway, go wash your hair."

"Hey before you hang up, Celeste, you need to explain your voicemail to me. Did you really get a tattoo on your—"

Darn it. My phone's died. I remind myself to dig the charger out of my backpack later, then get busy washing the hair dye . . . not to mention that Frenchman . . . right out of my hair.

* * *

When I walk into the kitchen, I catch Jean-Paul and Amélie mid-kiss. It's both awkward and sweet. I don't mean that they're awkward. They're adorable. Married for so long and still obviously in love. That part is sweet. I'm the one that feels awkward, interrupting their affectionate moment.

Before I can tiptoe out, Amélie spots me. She motions at the kitchen table. "Come sit and have an apéritif while I finish chopping the vegetables. Jean-Paul, go get her a drink."

Jean-Paul pours some pastis into a glass, then adds water, which changes the color of the anise-flavored liqueur from yellow to a milky-white. When he hands the glass to me, he does a double take. "Your hair is blue."

Amélie smiles at me. "It looks lovely. *Très chic*."

Twisting my hair into a knot, I look at her uncertainly. "I'm not sure it's *chic*."

"Oh, yes, it's very *chic*," she says. "You have a natural sense of style. Madame Toussaint was saying as much the other day."

"Pierre's mother thinks I'm stylish?"

"Yes. That surprises you?" She places a bowl of potatoes in front of me to peel. "You need to believe in yourself more, *chérie."*

I take a sip of my pastis, then get to work on the potatoes.

Jean-Paul looks at me thoughtfully. "How did you react when Pierre told you that you were beautiful?"

I snort. "Beautiful? Me? Pierre? None of those things go together in a sentence."

"But he thinks you're beautiful. He told me that."

"Well, he never said that to me." I take another sip of my drink, savoring the intense licorice flavor.

"Hmm . . . I thought he had," Jean-Paul says.

While the three of us work quietly preparing the ingredients for our dinner, I think back to the night of the charity ball. Pierre had tried to kiss me in front of everyone. When I tried to stop him, he said something about there being nothing wrong with kissing a beautiful woman in public. Am I remembering that right? Did he call *me* beautiful?

"Okay, I'll show you how to make the Béarnaise sauce now," Amélie says.

While she demonstrates how to emulsify egg yolks and butter with vinegar, Jean-Paul inquires about whether Pierre asked me to be on the Board of Trustees for his charity yet.

I nearly drop the sprig of tarragon I'm holding. "Excuse me?"

"Yes, he was going to ask you once he got the paperwork back from his lawyer."

"Paperwork . . . lawyer . . ." I splutter, feeling my face grow warm as I remember the prenuptial fiasco.

Amélie takes the herbs out of my hand. "Pierre was very impressed with the charity work you did in the States. Imagine, helping former gang members like that by covering up their tattoos."

"Pierre said that you take symbols of hate and turn them into something else," Jean-Paul says. "How exactly do you do that?"

I shrug. "It just takes some creativity, I guess. I talk with the guys, ask them for their ideas, and draw some designs for them to consider. Then I get to work."

"But it's not work, is it?" Jean-Paul asks. "You do it for free."

"Well, sure. These guys are trying to make a fresh start in life. All it takes on my part is time. It's really no big deal."

Amélie shakes her head. "It is a big deal. Not everyone would work with people like that."

"Everyone needs a second chance," I say.

Jean-Paul seasons some steaks, then places them on a hot cast iron grill. "Pierre said that you do more than tattoo cover-ups. You also work with communities and raise money to help ex-convicts get a fresh start."

"You know, I need to go make a call." I tug at my collar while I inch toward the door. "Can you let me know when dinner is ready?"

Amélie calls after me. "Remember what you said about everyone deserving a second chance? Maybe you should call Pierre."

CHAPTER 14
YELLOW-BELLIED MARMOTS

Birds chirping outside my bedroom window wake me the next morning. A light breeze makes the lace curtains flutter, and sunlight dances around the room. Stretching my arms above my head, I'm tempted to crawl back under the covers, but my stomach has other ideas, namely to be fed.

I'm surprised at how hungry I am, especially after the huge dinner I had. The French have managed to take a simple meal of steak and fries and elevate it to an art form. Add in red wine, salad, and chocolate mousse for dessert, and you can see why people who visit Paris never want to leave.

Do I want to leave Paris, especially after everything that's happened with Pierre? I'm really going to need to figure out the answer to that question. Last night, Amélie made me promise that I would stay and work at the art gallery until the end of summer. After that, the tourist season will wind down and the tattoo photography exhibition will be over. Then, I'll be free to leave Paris . . . if that's what I really want.

My stomach growls so loudly that the birds on the windowsill startle and fly away. When I check the time on my phone, I'm surprised that it's after ten. I can't remember the last time I slept in so late. No wonder I'm hungry.

Before setting my phone back on the nightstand, I check my texts, emails, and voice messages. Nothing from

Pierre. Did he check his phone as well this morning to see if I had tried to contact him? Amélie had told me that I should give him a second chance and reach out to him, but I can't. Not yet. What would I say? There's so much I need to figure out first, on my own, starting with whether I want to make a life in Paris long-term. Besides, don't second chances work both ways? Does he want to give me one too?

The sound of my stomach growling drowns out my thoughts about Pierre. Giving in to hunger, I get dressed and head into the kitchen. While the coffee brews, I read the note Jean-Paul left for me on the table. "There's more to life than work. Go enjoy all that Paris has to offer."

Underneath the note is a large envelope with my name scrawled on it. When I open it, I find a walking map of the city and a guidebook, along with complimentary tickets to the Eiffel

Tower and a boat ride on the Seine. I smile. Jean-Paul knows that, despite having lived in Paris for a few months, I've actually seen very little of the city. When I haven't been working, I've been sleeping. And when I haven't been sleeping, I've been working. Today, things are going to change. It's time to experience the City of Lights like a tourist.

After a quick breakfast of yogurt and fruit—I promise my stomach I'll feed it more later—I grab my map and head to my first stop, the Arc de Triomphe. When I get there, I'm struck by the grandeur of the memorial arch that honors soldiers who fought and died for France. I pause for a moment at the eternal flame near the tomb of an unknown soldier from World War I and give a moment of silent thanks for people who make the ultimate sacrifice serving their country.

Next, I stroll down the famed Avenue

des Champs-Élysées toward the Place de la Concorde. The trees which line the avenue remind me of rectangular lollipops, the luxury clothing shops remind me of Giselle and her friends, and the cafes remind me that it's almost lunchtime. Waiters try to entice me to sit at one of the outdoor tables and enjoy a meal, but given my financial situation, I'm going to have to settle for a sandwich from a food stand instead.

An Egyptian obelisk stands at the center of the Place de la Concorde. Munching on a crusty baguette filled with ham and cheese, I examine the hieroglyphics on the large granite column. The Toussaint family owns a hotel in Cairo, a place I've always wanted to visit. Seeing the pyramids, exploring the Egyptian Museum, and shopping in a souq—these are all things on my bucket list. Maybe traveling to Egypt is what I should do next with my life. Obviously, I could never afford to stay at Pierre's family's hotel there, but I'm sure there are nice hostels in my price range.

The Louvre isn't far from the Place de la Concorde, but I decide to skip a return visit. It would remind me too much of Pierre. Instead, I walk down to the Seine and board one of the hop on and off tourist boats. The next hour passes by quickly. I learn a few interesting tidbits along the way, including the fact that there's only one stop sign in the entire city. I wonder if that's why the traffic is so crazy here. If I were a billionaire like Pierre, I'd definitely have a chauffeur drive me around everywhere. That would be a perk of being rich that I'd definitely enjoy.

As the boat nears the Eiffel Tower, I snap a few pictures of the most recognizable landmark in Paris. The line for tickets snakes around the block. Thankfully, the ticket Jean-Paul gave me gives me VIP access to the elevators to the top. I suppose one of the perks of being a concierge is getting complimentary tickets like these, and it was sweet of him to pass it along to me.

The elevator takes me to the second level. The views of Paris are amazing from here, and I even dare to walk out on the glass floor, which is eighteen stories above street level. Looking down, I experience a bit of vertigo, but nothing like I would have felt in the past. Skydiving seems to have cured me of not only a fear of flying but also a fear of heights.

Next, I board another elevator for the top of the tower. The views are even more stunning. I lean against the railing and try to make out famous landmarks.

"Hello, Mia," I hear an American woman say behind me. I turn around in dread, expecting to see one of the snobby ladies from the country club back home. Instead, I find myself face to face with Pierre's mother. She's impeccably dressed as ever—a sheath dress with an abstract floral print, pink stilettos, and amethysts dangling from her ears.

I'm having a hard time reconciling her fashionable Parisian attire with her flat American accent. Shouldn't she have a posh British accent like Pierre?

"Madame Toussaint," I splutter.

"Please, call me Gladys."

"Gladys? That's not a very French name," I blurt out.

"That's probably because I'm not French," she says, her eyes crinkling with amusement. "I'm American. Born and bred in North Dakota."

* * *

I blink rapidly, trying to recover my power of speech. The elegant woman standing in front of me is Gladys of North Dakota. Or, as they would say in

France, Gladys de Dakota du Nord.

"Okay, let me see if I have this straight," I say. "You're originally from one of those rectangular states in the middle of the country."

She smiles, an expression I'm not used to seeing on her. "Yes, the rectangular state near the Canadian border."

"But, how . . . how . . ." My voice trails off. I don't even know where to begin. How did Gladys end up in France? How did she end up married to Pierre's father? Is it really so cold in North Dakota that people have to plug their cars in?

"My dad had a block heater on one of his cars," she says. "He'd plug it in before he started it in the winter. It helped."

"Oh, I guess I asked those questions out loud." Pierre's mother nods, and I press my fingers to my temples. I really need to get better at keeping my internal monologues inside my head where they belong. This whole talking out loud thing keeps getting me in trouble.

"Why don't we have a drink and I'll answer the rest of your questions?"

As she points at the entrance to the Bar à Champagne, I look around expecting her poodle to come barreling around the corner any minute and growl at me. "Where's your dog?"

"Lyonette? She's at home, tuckered out from playing in the park earlier."

"I suppose she's from North Dakota too."

"No, she's from the south of France. I adopted her from a dog rescue organization near Carcossonne. It's the same place we're raising money for with the photography exhibition that you're working on."

"She's a rescue dog?"

"Yes, poor thing was abused, then abandoned by her previous owner. She's come a long way since we've had her, but she still gets skittish at times. And when she gets overexcited, she sometimes plays too roughly. Like she did with you that day in the art gallery. I still feel terrible about how she ripped your blouse."

I chew on my lip. Not only have I made assumptions about Pierre's mother that weren't right, I've also misjudged her dog. Lyonette isn't some snooty, high-strung poodle. She's been abused and abandoned, and is having to learn how to trust humans again.

"Come on, you look like you could use that drink," Gladys says.

I follow her into the bar and wince when I see the prices. "I'm not really thirsty."

"Nonsense. You can't pass up bubbles at the top of the Eiffel Tower." She orders two glasses of pink champagne, paying for them before I can protest. "It's my treat."

"Really," I say. "I can buy my own

drink."

I unzip my backpack and pull my wallet out. She shakes her head, the stern look on her face reminding me that this isn't just Gladys from North Dakota. This is also Madame Toussaint, the directrice d'Hôtel de la Marmotte. "Pierre told me that you feel uncomfortable when people buy things for you."

"He did?"

"I used to feel the same way with Pierre's father. When we first started dating, he was constantly showering me with gifts." Her expression softens. "He swept into my life, and swept me off my feet."

"How did you meet? Was it in North Dakota?"

"No, by the time we met, I was living in Montana, working at a hotel near Yellowstone National Park."

"The hotel was owned by the Toussaint family?"

"It is now. That's why he was there, to acquire it. Initially, he traveled back and forth from France, but once the deal was complete, he moved to Montana to take over the day-to-day management of the hotel." She takes a sip of her champagne, then fiddles with her wedding band. "That was a wonderful time in our lives. We'd both work hard during the week, then the three of us would go hiking in the park on the weekends."

"The three of you? Pierre was there too?"

"Oh, yes. Pierre had been attending boarding school in Britain, but his father thought having him spend time in the States would be a good opportunity for him. He arranged for a private tutor for him so that he could keep up with his studies, but, between you and me, I think Pierre learned almost as much through his time exploring the outdoors and nature."

She asks the waiter to bring us some more champagne. "Would you like some caviar too?"

I wrinkle my nose. "Fish eggs?"

"Never had it?"

I shake my head.

"I'll order some. If you don't think about the fact that its salmon roe, I think you'll be pleasantly surprised at how good it tastes."

"Really?"

"Absolutely. I remember the first time Pierre tried caviar. I think he was nine or ten at the time. He wasn't convinced either, but now he loves it."

"Tell me more about what he was like as a kid," I say.

She spoons caviar onto a toast point and hands it to me. "The first time he saw a yellow-bellied marmot, he was so excited. He became obsessed with them, begging his father to get him one as a pet. He kept trying to explain to Pierre that they were wild animals who needed to live freely in nature. Pierre was despondent. So, I made him his own stuffed marmot."

"What are we talking about? Taxidermy? I guess that's the type of thing you do in North Dakota and Montana during the long winters."

She laughs. "No, I sewed one for him out of felt. He loved it. He would take it everywhere with him. He even tried to take it into the tub with him at bath time until we explained that Frank didn't like to swim."

"Frank?"

"Yes, Frank the Marmot. Don't ask me where he got the name Frank from." She glances at the plate in front of me. "You haven't tried your caviar yet. Go on, give it a chance."

I slowly lift the toast point to my mouth and nibble the edge of it. I feel tiny ocean-flavored bubbles pop on my tongue. It tastes slightly salty, slightly fishy, and a hundred percent delicious.

"You're right, it is good."

"I'm not right about everything, but when it comes to caviar, I do know what I'm talking about." She hands me another toast point, which I quickly devour. "I knew someone like you would love the taste of fish eggs."

The taste of caviar turns sour in my mouth. "Someone like me? You think I'm a gold digger, don't you?"

Gladys frowns. "A gold digger? Not at all. Some of the more obnoxious people in Pierre's circle might call a woman a gold-digger if they thought she was after his money. But that'd be the last thing I'd ever say about anyone. Especially not after what I experienced after I married Pierre's father."

I lean forward. "What happened?"

"Listen, I'm a girl like you. I grew up in a small town. My parents worked hard, but we didn't have a lot of money growing up. I couldn't have told you the difference between a fish fork and a salad fork. And I certainly had never eaten fish eggs before." She pauses to sample the caviar, sighing in appreciation. "Anyway, after I married Pierre's father, we moved back to France. That's when I discovered that many members of Parisian high society considered me to be some sort of upstart country bumpkin who was only after his money."

"Oh, my gosh, that's awful. What did you do?"

She narrows her eyes. "I adapted. I learned how to speak French fluently, doing my best to lose all traces of my American accent. In fact, I rarely speak English these days. This is the first time in a long time."

"That can't have been easy."

She shrugs. "I was determined to be the perfect French wife. The clothes, the hair and make-up; things like that were easy. But getting people to accept me, that took time." When she fixes her gaze on me, I notice that her eyes are hazel, just like Pierre's. "So, you see, I'd be the last person to accuse you of being a gold-digger. No, that's not what I was worried about with you."

"What were you worried about?" I ask, not sure that I want to know the answer.

"My close friends call me a lioness. I'll do anything to protect the people I love. Pierre had been terribly hurt by another woman, and I didn't want to see that happen to him again."

"Let me guess, Giselle?"

She taps the side of her nose. "Correct. She's a piece of work. A liar and a cheater. I kept telling Pierre that he shouldn't trust her, but he didn't believe me. You know Giselle was married before, don't you?"

I shake my head.

"Pierre didn't, either. Turns out she had met some guy when she was traveling in Brazil, took a fancy to him, and married him. I guess he was gorgeous, but dumb as a rock."

"Are you saying she had a boytoy?"

"That's one way of putting it. Her secret boytoy. She never told any of her friends and family that she had gotten married. Eventually, she got bored with him, and came back to France for a while. Pierre had just come back from Africa and the two of them starting spending time together. Then one day, a gossip magazine discovered Giselle's secret husband. It's the kind of juicy scandal they love to print. Pierre was furious when the article came out. She laughed it off, saying that the Brazilian guy didn't mean anything to her."

"I can see how Pierre would be upset that Giselle was cheating on her husband."

"But it was more than that," Gladys says. "It was also the fact that Giselle abandoned the poor guy, like a dog abandons a toy they've tired of. When it came time to do his rotation as a waiter, he decided he needed to get out of

Paris and away from Giselle."

"That explains a lot." I twirl a lock of my hair, then stifle a laugh. I had forgotten that I had dyed it blue. Earlier today, I would have been worried about what Pierre's mother would think of my hair color, but now that I've gotten to know Gladys de Dakota du Nord, things are different. I take a deep breath, then say, "I was married once. When Pierre found out about it, well . . ."

"He was angry," she says quietly.

"He told you?"

"No, he hasn't said anything to me. Amélie told me what happened." She cocks her head to one side. "I had an impulse to visit the Eiffel Tower today. It's not normally something I would do, but I was drawn here for some reason. And I think that reason was you. It was a chance to get to know you."

I raise my glass and clink it against hers. "And for me to get to know you too."

CHAPTER 15
A STAR WARS TANGENT

I tell Gladys everything about my short-lived marriage. She listens intently. There's no judgment, only understanding. Eventually, I run out of steam and out of stories. The experience has left me feeling lighter and deeply relaxed, almost like I've had a gentle massage at a spa.

As we part ways at the bottom of the Eiffel Tower, Gladys tells me that Pierre can be stubborn. "You'll have to be the one to reach out to him. After what happened with Giselle, he'll be skittish about trusting you."

I take her hands and squeeze them. "I do care for your son, but I'm not sure that's enough. I know you were able to adapt to this world, but I can't do that. I don't *want* to do that. Pierre and I weren't meant to be together. We need different things out of life."

"Nonsense. You two are perfect for each other. Once you and my son have a heart-to-heart, you'll see that too." She kisses me on the cheek, then gets into her car. Before the chauffeur closes the door, she adds, "You just have to believe, Mia."

As her car speeds away, I pull my phone out. So much has happened that I can't process it. I feel like my head is going to explode. It's time for a debrief with the girls.

Isabelle is the first to dial into the video chat. I turn my phone around so she can see the Eiffel Tower.

"What was it like at the top?" she asks.

"Full of fish eggs and bubbles," I say.

She laughs. "You say the weirdest things."

Ginny pops on. "What did I miss?"

"Mia is at the Eiffel Tower," Isabelle says.

"Did you know that a man cycled down the stairs in 1923 for a bet?" Ginny asks. "He won the bet, but the police arrested him at the bottom."

"How do you keep all those random history tidbits in your brain?" I ask.

Before Ginny can answer, I hear Celeste say, "How do I get this to work again?"

"You're pointing your phone at the floor, Celeste," I say. "Turn it around . . . there you go."

Celeste waves at us once she gets into view. "Hello, girls. Ooh, Mia, I love your hair. Blue really suits you."

"It suits my mood," I say.

"You still haven't patched things up

with Pierre?" Celeste asks. "You really should."

"You sound just like his mother."

Ginny arches an eyebrow. "His mother? You mean the Ice Queen of France?"

"Turns out she's not as icy as I thought."

After I fill them in on my tête-à-tête with Gladys, Isabelle asks me what I'm going to do about Pierre. "Do you think his mom is right about the two of you belonging together?"

"Look, I'll be the first to admit that there's something between the two of us —"

Celeste chortles. "Something? A little something called love, that's what it is." Then she starts humming a show tune.

"*South Pacific*?" I ask.

"No, *Oklahoma*," she says.

I shake my head. "Never seen it."

"Well, here's what we're going to do, dear. I'm going to send you a ticket to

Greece. You come visit, we'll watch *Oklahoma*, and we'll sort out your love life. It worked for Ginny. She had some baklava, we watched *To Catch a Thief*, and now she's with the guy she was always meant to be with."

"That's sweet, Celeste, but I can't go to Greece. The photography exhibition opens next week, and I promised Amélie that I'd work at the art gallery until the end of the summer."

"Well, I'll pop a ticket in the mail, just in case you change your mind."

"No, really, even if I could come to Greece, I would never let you buy my ticket."

Isabelle pipes up. "Mia has a hard time accepting gifts from people."

"My, oh my, if that isn't the craziest thing I ever heard," Celeste says. "What do you do on Christmas? Sit in the corner and play with crumpled up wrapping paper like a cat while everyone else opens up their presents?"

"No, that's different," I say.

"How so?"

"Um, I spend Christmas with my family and friends."

Celeste gives me a mischievous smile. "So gifts from friends are okay?"

Realizing I've been trapped in a corner, I quickly end the call, promising to touch base again with them after the photography exhibition.

* * *

A couple of days later, I get a cryptic phone call from Dominic de Santis asking if I can meet him at Voodoo Hoodoo that evening. The timing works well for me. I start work back at the art gallery tomorrow, and it'll be crazy busy putting the finishing touches on the photography exhibition. There will be little enough time to eat and sleep, let alone to visit the coolest tattoo parlor in Paris.

I spend the day puttering around Jean-Paul and Amélie's apartment, then grab my backpack and walk to the Métro. Some people turn up their nose at public transportation, but I enjoy it. The buskers playing music outside the station, the eccentric characters sitting next to you on the train, the diversity of languages being spoken—it all adds to the vibe that is Paris.

When I get to the tattoo parlor, Dominic greets me enthusiastically. "Your hair is fabulous. And your outfit is to die for. Now, come along. I want to get your advice about something."

"Me? My advice?"

"Yes, of course. That's why I asked you to come here." Snapping his fingers, he instructs his assistant to pour us some sparkling water, then grabs my hand. As he leads me toward the rear of the tattoo parlor, he tells me that everyone who is everyone is going to be at the opening night of the exhibition.

"You will raise lots of money for those poor abandoned dogs. I'm thinking of adopting one. I have my eye on the most adorable Chihuahua."

When he pushes open the door to the back room, I gasp. Lying on the table is a man with a very familiar-looking back. Gazing at the elephant tattoo at the base of his neck and the yellow-bellied marmot tattoo on his right shoulder, I put my hands on my hips. "What exactly is going on here, Dominic?"

"I thought that would have been obvious." He points at the rock that the marmot is sitting on. "I need to finish this portion of the tattoo, and I want to get your advice on how to do the shading."

Yeah, right. A world-renown celebrity tattoo artist wants my advice on something as basic as shading? Not very likely. "This is a set-up. Who put you up to this?"

Pierre rolls over on his side, giving me a view of his sculpted abs. He fixes his eyes on Dominic. "Please tell me my mother didn't have anything to do with this."

Dominic puts his hand to his chest in mock horror. "I don't know what you two think is going on here. I simply wanted to get the advice of a colleague on your tattoo."

"I bet it was Amélie," I say.

"Where is that girl with the sparkling water? I'm dying of thirst. I'm going to track her down." Dominic waves his hand at us. "I'll leave the two of you to discuss the marmot tattoo."

Pierre sits up on the table and runs his fingers through his hair. I want nothing more than to rush over and run my own fingers through his sandy-brown locks. The last time I touched his hair, it was incredibly soft. I'm dying to find out what conditioning product he uses, but that would seem like a weird question to ask in this particular moment.

Instead, I lean against the wall,

maintaining a safe distance between the two of us. "Do you think he's coming back with water?"

Pierre suppresses a smile. "I highly doubt it."

"Do you really think your mother arranged for us to run into each other here?" I ask.

"I hope not," he says. "She still doesn't know that I have tattoos."

"Do you really think she'd be upset by them?"

"Yeah." He sighs. "Ever since I can remember, she told me that people with tattoos lack class. She can be a real snob sometimes. I've tried to tell her a million times that tattoos are mainstream now, but she's got a real hang-up about it. I don't know why."

"It probably has to do with what she experienced when she moved to Paris."

"Why do you think that?" Pierre asks, his brow furrowed.

"It couldn't have been easy being an

American from a small town, suddenly finding herself thrown into French high society. She told me about—"

Pierre pushes himself off the table and takes a step toward me. "You spoke with my mother?"

"Uh, yeah . . ."

He narrows his eyes. "When?"

"A few days ago." I fold my arms across my chest, unsure why he's so agitated. "I ran into her at the top of the Eiffel Tower. Gladys and I had a good chat over champagne and caviar."

Pierre scrubs a hand across his chin, then bursts out laughing. "She told you her real name is Gladys? Wow, I think you're the first person outside of me and my father who knows that. She insists on being called Juliette."

"Like I said, we had a good chat. Turns out we have a lot in common. We're both from small towns, grew up on the wrong side of the tracks, and . . . "

Pierre takes another step forward, closing the gap between the two of us. "And what?"

"Nothing," I mumble, lowering my gaze and squeezing my arms tighter around my chest.

"Tell me," he says as he softly strokes my cheek. When I don't respond, he gently kisses the top of my head, then trails kisses down my face, pausing to nibble on my earlobe. He slips his fingers underneath the collar of my blouse and pulls it back slightly. I gasp as he brushes his lips against my neck. He draws back and looks intently at me, his hazel eyes sparkling in the overhead light. "Tell me."

Snaking my fingers through the belt loops of his jeans, I pull him back toward me. I run my hands up his bare chest, then loop them around the back of his neck. As he bends his head down to kiss me, I whisper, "And we both fell in love with French guys."

"Love," he murmurs, his lips brushing against mine. "You love me?"

"Yes, I love you." Then I start giggling. Totally inappropriate for the moment, I know.

When Pierre looks at me quizzically, I explain. "Sorry. That scene from *The Empire Strikes Back* is playing in my head. The one where Princess Leia tells Han Solo that she loves him right before he's about to be encased in carbonite and he replies, 'I know.'"

Pierre gives me a cocky grin. "Despite the fact that I own a Han Solo costume, I'm no Han Solo—"

"You don't have to tell me that," I say with a teasing tone. "You're not nearly as good of a spaceship pilot as he is."

He puts a finger on my lips. "Let me finish. What I was going to say is that you should tell me you love me again and wait for my reply without going off on some *Star Wars* tangent."

"*Star Wars* tangent? Me? Never." I

hold my hands up in a mocking surrender fashion. My mouth grows dry as he grabs my wrists and presses me against the wall. As his lips near mine, I groan before uttering the words, "I love you."

"I love you too," he says, then kisses the side of my mouth.

As his kisses become more intense, the door flies open. Dominic's assistant is standing there with a tray. "Monsieur de Santis said that you two wanted some water."

* * *

I'm mortified at being caught doing the smoochy-face thing. I grab the tray from Dominic's assistant and practically run into the reception area. After setting the tray on the coffee table, I sink onto the red velvet couch.

Pierre sits next to me and takes a sip of water. "That tastes good. It was getting hot in there, don't you think?"

My face feels flushed. I grab a glass and gulp down its contents. Then I burp. So ladylike, I know. But when you drink water that's carbonated really quickly, well, sometimes things go terribly wrong.

Pierre laughs, and I smack him playfully. He pours me some more water, which I sip more slowly this time.

"So, we should probably talk," I say.

"Talk. That sounds serious. Wouldn't you rather go back into that room and talk about my tattoo some more?" He winks. "And by 'talk about my tattoo,' I mean—"

I hold my hand up. "I know exactly what you mean. But I think we've had enough tattoo talk for right now. Although, there is one tattoo-related question I have."

Pierre points toward the back room. "Shall we?"

"I think we can discuss it out here," I

say with a smile.

"Okay, shoot." Pierre leans back in the couch.

"It has to do with your scar. Dominic has done an amazing job incorporating it into the marmot tattoo. So naturally, I want to know how you got the scar."

He quirks an eyebrow. "Naturally."

"Jean-Paul told me that you had an injury which put an end to playing rugby in college. I assume this scar has something to do with it?" When he nods, I add, "I've figured out most of your secrets, but I still don't know the story behind this one."

"Secrets? I don't have any secrets from you."

"Hah. When I met you, you were a waiter. You never told me you were a billionaire. That's a pretty big secret."

Pierre runs his fingers around the rim of his glass. After a beat, he takes my hand in his. "Listen, I get that the fact that I come from money is a big deal to you, but it's not what defines me. I wasn't drawn to you because of your financial status. When I first met you, I was attracted to the fact that you were a *Star Wars* geek like me."

"You weren't attracted to me because of how gorgeous I am?" I say in a mocking tone.

His expression grows serious. "Mia, that goes without saying. You are incredibly beautiful."

"As beautiful as Giselle?" As I utter those words, I realize how pathetic I sound.

"Sure, Giselle is pretty, if you like that kind of thing. But you're . . . you're . . . beautiful inside and out." He runs his fingers through his hair. "You'll have to excuse me. I'm not very good with this kind of thing. My parents are both really reserved. We never really talk about feelings and—"

Now Pierre looks like the one who's mortified. As his face reddens, I take pity on him and try to lighten the mood. "Wow, this is really getting sappy, mister. Sorry, I was just having an insecure moment because I know about you and Giselle's history."

He cocks his head to one side. "You do?"

"Yep, Gladys told me all about it."

"I'm going to have to have a word with her." He shakes his head, then says, "Just believe me when I say that you're beautiful, okay? And we'll leave it at that."

"Believe," I say softly.

Pierre claps his hands together. "Okay, what else do you want to know? What other secrets do you think I'm hiding from you?"

"Well, there's the Board of Trustees thing. What was that all about?"

"Oh, that." Pierre purses his lips. "There were a lot of misunderstandings the day we went skydiving, weren't there? You thought I was going to propose, when what I was planning on doing was asking you to join the board of my charity. I really think we can benefit from your experience with grassroots fundraising, and you'd bring a fresh perspective to the work we do."

"Yeah, that whole prenuptial thing was pretty embarrassing."

He takes a deep breath. "And I'm embarrassed about how I reacted when I found out you had been married before. Amélie told me all about your ex and what a jerk he and his family were to you. I shouldn't have jumped to conclusions."

"Hmm, so Amélie told you about my ex and your mother filled me in on Giselle? They're a couple of busybodies, aren't they?"

"The best kind of busybodies, don't you think? If it hadn't been for them, we wouldn't be here right now." He reaches for my hand and gently kisses the back of it. "Was that okay? I know you're not a big fan of public displays of affection."

I rub my thumb on the palm of his hand. "I'm starting to get used to them. Now, about that scar."

He laughs. "Not everything is a juicy secret. Some are just embarrassing. When I was in college, I went to a panel at a *Star Wars* convention. Some really big cast members were on stage. I was standing on a wobbly chair, trying to take pictures of them. This die-hard fan wearing a Wookie costume rushed the stage. Security was running after him, and I got knocked down."

"Ouch," I say. "You must have landed on something sharp."

"Yep. I had a replica of the knife Han Solo used in the original *Star Wars* movie. Turns out those things aren't made out of plastic. I ended up needing surgery, so I was out of rugby for the rest of the season."

I squeeze his hand. "Oh, you poor thing."

"You want to kiss it and make it better?" he asks with a wink.

I pour him some more water instead, and we spend the rest of the evening talking about marmots, *Star Wars*, and skydiving.

CHAPTER 16
BELIEVE

"Everything looks wonderful, *chérie*," Amélie says.

I look around the art gallery with a critical eye. It's the night of the opening reception for the photography exhibition. There's nothing more I can do. The photographs have been hung, the catalog has been printed, and the catering is set up. Now, all that remains is to open the doors and let the guests in.

I spend the evening making sure

glasses are filled with champagne, answering questions about the work on display, and handing out brochures about the animal shelter that we're raising funds for. I even arrange for some dogs to be adopted. Dominic will be providing a home to not one, but two Chihuahuas, and Pierre's mother has taken a liking to a German Shepard-Beauceron cross.

Giselle is there too. She shows an interest in the picture of a bichon frise puppy, but I tell her the dog isn't available. He is, but Giselle is the type of person who has pets because they look cute in her handbag, not because she has a genuine interest in their well being.

I can tell that she's annoyed with me because I hear her tell her friends that my unsophisticated American palate could never appreciate escargot. Giving her a haughty look, I snatch one of the slimy snails from a tray and pop it into my mouth. I'm prepared to smile my way through this disgusting morsel when, to my surprise, I discover that escargot are delicious. Garlic and butter —what's not to love?

I grab a few more and put them on a plate along with some other hors d'oeuvres. Roaming around the gallery, I see Pierre standing with his mother in front of the photographs that were taken at the Voodoo Hoodoo the day Dominic was inking a marmot on Pierre's shoulder.

I have to confess that I eavesdrop on their conversation. Gladys recognizes Pierre's back. At first, she's taken aback that he had gotten a tattoo of an elephant without telling her. He explains to her that it was a reminder of the work that he does with African orphanages. She purses her lips, then her expression softens when he tells her that the yellow-bellied marmot is in her honor, of the day she said yes to his father's proposal and became not only his dad's wife but also Pierre's mother.

Slipping away unnoticed, I mingle among the guests. As a couple from Sri Lanka tell me that they want to buy the photographs which were taken at the Voodoo Hoodoo, a woman asks for everyone's attention.

"Mia, Mia, where are you?" Amélie calls out. I raise my hand meekly. "Come up here, please."

As I make my way to join her, Jean-Paul congratulates me on the success of the reception

When I get to the front of the art gallery, Amélie hands me a glass of champagne. She raises her own glass and makes a toast. "I want to thank Mia, the talented young woman from America, who is responsible for this evening. This exhibition wouldn't have happened without her. The Galérie d'Art Animalier are lucky to have her."

As I take a sip of champagne, Pierre's

mother makes her way through the crowd.

When she reaches me, she says in English, "It's not just the Galérie d'Art Animalier who are fortunate to have Mia. It is also everyone at the Hôtel de la Marmotte who are grateful to have her in our midst. And now I would like to present her with a small token of our gratitude."

As a bellboy presents me with a yellow duckie, I grin at Gladys de Dakota du Nord.

* * *

Pierre grabs my hand. "Come with me."

As he leads me toward the back room, I laugh. "No, I don't think so, mister. We can't go play smoochy-face while there's a reception happening out here."

"Making out with you?" He shakes his head. "That is the last thing I had on my mind."

"Yeah, sure," I say. Then I do a double take. "Wait a minute, are you saying you don't want to kiss me? What? Do I have escargot between my teeth?"

He laughs. "This has nothing to do with snails. No, I have something for you back here."

"Okay," I say dubiously.

"Sit here," he says, pointing at a stool in the corner. Then he reaches behind the canvases stacked in the corner and pulls out a large box.

"What's that?"

"It's called a present. Can't you tell from the awesome gift wrapping?"

He places the box on the table behind me. I swivel my stool around and smile when I see the R2-D2 and C-3PO pattern on the wrapping paper. "What is it?"

"You don't seem to be very familiar with how presents work." He taps the large gold bow on top of the box. "You remove the ribbon, tear the paper off, and rip the box open to reveal its contents."

I do as he recommends—untying ribbon, tearing paper, and ripping the box open. My eyes widen when I see what's inside. "Is this what I think it is?"

"Again, confused about how this process works. After opening the box, you remove the object inside and inspect it."

I chew on my lip, undecided about what to do.

Pierre leans down and whispers in my ear. "It's just a present. It doesn't mean anything other than the fact that I love you. I'm not trying to control you or buy you off. Although, if you like it, a thank-you kiss wouldn't go amiss."

As I gingerly pull Pierre's gift out of the box, a huge smile creeps across my face. "This is a custom-made lightsaber."

"Don't forget the titanium handle," he says. "Do you like it?"

"Like it? I love it." I hop down from the stool and swing the lightsaber back and forth. "Oh, my gosh, it feels fantastic."

"I'm glad you like it." Pierre grins and taps his cheek. "Does it deserve a kiss?"

"Let me think about it." I twirl around, sweeping the lightsaber in circles around me. Mesmerized by the way the light glistens off the blade, I'm oblivious to where I'm pointing my lightsaber. A crashing noise startles me, and I yelp as a ceramic statue tumbles off the table.

Pierre dives, sliding across the floor, and catching it just inches before it would have been smashed into smithereens. After he places it back on the table, I set my lightsaber against the stool. Standing on my tiptoes, I plant a kiss on his cheek. "Thank you, I love it."

He turns my head toward me and brushes his lips gently against mine. "And I love you."

After a few minutes of toe-curling

kisses, I say, "There's something I wanted to show you." He winks as I unbutton the sleeve of my blouse. "No, silly, it's not that. It's this."

He lifts my wrist and smiles. "Is that what I think it is? A tattoo?"

"Uh-huh. Dominic did it for me the other night. See what it says?"

Pierre traces his fingers gently around the tattoo. "Believe."

"That word means a lot to me," I say. "Believe in myself, believe in my dreams, and believe in—"

Pierre finishes my sentence for me. "Believe in love."

Then we play smoochy-face.

EPILOGUE
PIERRE

I furrow my brow as Mia adjusts the straps on her parachute. "Make sure they're tight."

Mia smiles at me. "Stop fussing. I know what I'm doing. It's been almost a year since I did my first tandem jump with you, and I've had plenty of training and practice since then."

"It's been *exactly* one year since that first time we went skydiving together," I say. "This is our skydiving anniversary."

"I don't know if that's a day we want to

celebrate." Mia frowns. "That fight we had was horrible."

"It was all my fault," I say. "I overreacted when you told me you had been married before."

"No, it was my fault. I shouldn't have sprung it on you like that." She squeezes my arm. "At least you didn't have an embarrassing misunderstanding like I did. Can you believe I thought you were going to propose to me when we landed?"

I suppress a smile. "Yeah. What a crazy idea, huh?"

"Enough rehashing of the past," Mia says. "It's time to jump out of a plane."

The door opens, cold air rushes in, and I feel goosebumps all over my body. The goosebumps aren't a new sensation—I feel them every time I'm about to skydive. But this time, they're a reminder of how nervous I am for this particular jump. This is the jump that could change everything.

I watch as Mia steps out of the plane. It's hard to believe that only a year ago she was afraid of flying. Now she can't wait to get back up in the air and go skydiving. As I follow her, a huge grin spreads across my face. Sharing my passion for skydiving with the woman I love is more than I could have ever hoped for.

After we land and remove our gear, Stefan walks toward us with a spaniel-mix puppy bounding alongside him.

"Who is this cutie-pie?" Mia asks.

"His name is Yoda," Stefan says.

"Yoda? I didn't think you were a *Star Wars* fan," Mia says.

Stefan shakes his head. "I'm not."

Mia cocks her head to one side. "Then why did you name your dog after a *Star Wars* character?"

"I didn't," Stefan says, giving me a sideways glance.

I clear my throat. "I named him. He came from the animal shelter."

"He's adorable," Mia says. "It's great that you're going to give him a good home."

"Um . . . I was hoping *we* would give him a good home." I nod at Stefan and he unclips Yoda's leash.

Mia gives me a quizzical look as the puppy runs toward her. She bends down and grins as he licks her repeatedly on the face. As she scratches Yoda's head, she asks, "What's this attached to his collar?"

"Why don't you have a look?" I take a deep breath while she unties the small velvet pouch from Yoda's collar. As she opens it, I kneel on the ground next to her. She gasps as she peeks inside.

"Is this what I think it is?" she asks.

Her hands are trembling, so I take the pouch from her and pull out a diamond ring. "Will you do me the honor of becoming my wife, Mia?"

She looks up at me, her eyes glistening with tears, and nods.

While I slip the ring onto her finger, Yoda runs in circles around the two of us, barking excitedly.

Mia laughs, then pulls the dog into her lap. "You didn't have to bribe me with a puppy. I would have said yes, anyway."

"But it didn't hurt, did it?" I rub the dog's silky ears. "He was one of a litter of three who were abandoned."

"You mean there are two other puppies who need homes? We should adopt them." When I raise my eyebrows, she quickly adds, "What should we name them? Leia and Luke? Or should we go with Han and Lando? Maybe Rey—"

I silence her with a gentle kiss. "Enough *Star Wars* talk."

She kisses me back, then says, "You know we're going to have a *Star Wars*-themed wedding, don't you?"

"I'd expect nothing less," I say dryly.

Then we play smoochy-face again.

AUTHOR'S NOTE

Thank you so much for reading my book! If you enjoyed it, I'd be grateful if you would consider leaving a short review on the site where you purchased it and/or on Goodreads. Reviews help other readers find my books while also encouraging me to keep writing.

The Smitten with Travel romantic comedy series is inspired by my experiences living as an ex-pat for many years in Scotland and New Zealand and my travels, including my own "happily ever after" when my now-husband and I eloped to Denmark, followed by our honeymoon in Paris.

France holds a special place in my heart, and not just because my hubby and I honeymooned there. I first traveled to Europe when I was eighteen and Paris was one of the highlights of that trip. The food (especially the croissants), the architecture, the museums, the fashion—it was amazing, if not a bit overwhelming, to a girl from Cleveland. I had the opportunity to see more of France in subsequent trips and fell in love with the southern part of the country. When I was writing this novel, my husband said, "Hey, remember when we ate cassoulet in Carcassonne? Remember how much we loved it? You should include that in your book." So I did. Because he was right. Cassoulet is to die for. Having it in the fairy-tale setting of Carcassonne? Even better.

I want to thank Scott Jacobson (my cassoulet-loving husband), Duwan Dunn, and Greg Sifford for beta reading. Their insightful suggestions and feedback were invaluable. Sophie-Leigh Robbins and Mary Kelly Reed reviewed the French passages in this manuscript and offered invaluable advice (any grammatical mistakes are, of course, mine). Many thanks as well to my editor, Beth Balmanno, for her keen eye and thoughtful edits.

And, of course, I couldn't do this without you —my wonderful readers. Your support and encouragement means everything. I love to hear from readers, so please feel free to drop me an email at: ellenjacobsonauthor@gmail.com.

ABOUT THE AUTHOR

Ellen Jacobson is a chocolate obsessed cat lover who writes cozy mysteries and romantic comedies. After working in Scotland and New Zealand for several years, she returned to the States, lived aboard a sailboat, traveled around in a tiny camper, and is now settled in a small town in northern Oregon with her husband and an imaginary cat named Simon.

Find out more at ellenjacobsonauthor.com

ALSO BY ELLEN JACOBSON

Smitten with Travel Romantic Comedies

Smitten with Ravioli
Smitten with Croissants
Smitten with Strudel
Smitten with Candy Canes
Smitten with Baklava

Mollie McGhie Cozy Sailing Mysteries

Robbery at the Roller Derby
Murder at the Marina
Bodies in the Boatyard
Poisoned by the Pier
Buried by the Beach
Dead in the Dinghy
Shooting by the Sea
Overboard on the Ocean
Murder aboard the Mistletoe

North Dakota Library Mysteries

Planning for Murder